THE UNIVERSE FOR THE TAKING?

"You want to go out with a club," said Cal Truant's father, "and beat the universe into submission. . . . You want to go slaying dragons . . ."

"You," said Cal, "talk like it was murder. It isn't murder when a soldier kills."

"Isn't it? The killing of a soldier is always justified?"

"Yes," cried Cal. "What would you have done when mom was alive if some scaly lizard of an Alien had come breaking in trying to kill her?"

"I would have fought, of course," said his father.

"Then what's wrong with what I want to do? What?"

"Alexander of Macedon," said his father, "and Jesus of Nazareth both founded empires, Cal. Where are the hosts of the Alexandrians today?"

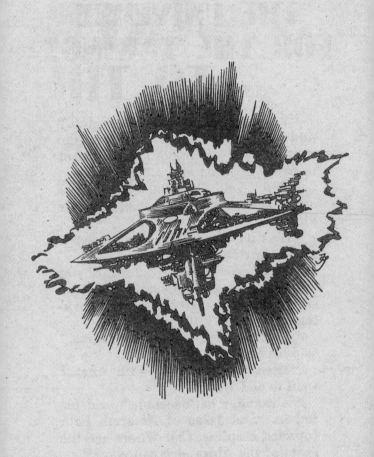

NAKED
TO THE
STARS

Gordon R. Dickson

DAW BOOKS, INC.

DONALD A. WOLLHEIM, PUBLISHER

1301 Avenue of the Americas
New York, N. Y.   10019

FIRST DAW PRINTING, JANUARY 1977

1 2 3 4 5 6 7 8 9

PRINTED IN U.S.A.

Chapter One

———◆———

The voice, speaking out of the ancient blackness of the night on the third planet of Arcturus—under an alien tree, bent and crippled by the remorseless wind—paused, and cleared its throat.

". . . ahem," it said. "Gentlemen . . ."

It seemed to lose its way for a second. It faltered and fell silent. Then it appeared to find strength and speak again:

". . . it's this way with the soldier. What makes the soldier different from the common, garden-variety murderer is the cause for which the soldier kills—" the voice broke off to clear its throat, which had become impeded by something soft and liquid.

"Bull!" said another voice, out of the wind-dry darkness.

"In a war," continued the first voice, unheeding, "to defend his hearth and family, for a crusade, during a definite limited time—the shield of high purpose and the feeling that his cause is just may be kept clean and bright. But soldiers become veterans—"

The voice broke off once more, on a liquid cough. It cleared its throat with effort.

"Some do. Yeah," said the second voice.

"—become veterans. And veterans become professional military men. So much so, that while it may remain a fine thing to let the enemy attack before the soldier goes to war, it becomes the practical thing to go to war first. When this happens, the aforementioned shield of high purpose, the heretofore unsullied escutcheon . . . ah . . ." the voice hesitated in its tone of impersonal dictation and muttered off into nonsense.

"Throw another nerve block into him, Joby," said Section Leader Calvin Truant, of the 4th Assault Wing, 91st Combat Engineers, Human Expedition against the Lehaunan.

"If I do," replied the voice that had been answering to the lecturing one, "I'll shove both thumbs through his spine. It's had it."

"Do it now," said Cal. There was a rustle, and the muttering broke off with a light gasp. There followed a moment's unnatural-seeming silence, then the voice resumed confidently.

". . . become veterans. And veterans become profess—with regard to the present situation of the Expedition, I can only report it as bogged down from the viewpoint of a Contacts Service Officer. Normally, at a time of truce we would expect to make considerable contact on the level of cultural understanding. However, it is by no means clear that the Lehaunan understand exactly what we mean by 'truce'—"

"You tell 'em!" said another, younger voice. "They were real trucy to you, weren't they, Runyon?"

"That's enough of that, Tack," said Cal. "Get back to the cable phone. See if Division hasn't got any orders for us yet."

"Right," said the younger voice. Cal heard feet moving off among the gravel and stones of the dark hillside along the side of the little hollow where they all lay, toward the eighty-three other men of what still called itself the 4th Assault Wing. In the nearly opposite direction, up the slope of the hollow, there was a faint glow in the night sky; a reflection of lights in the valley beyond where the small local community around the Lehaunan area Power Center was. The glow would have been invisible to any but men who had had no illumination but this for the past hours since the great orange orb of Arcturus had set.

". . . nor do they think of war in the same sense as we do, apparently. Although evidently capable of defending themselves, with great skill and effect against any powered attack, the Lehaunan appear largely ignorant of the idea of individual angers and hatreds. It appears almost as if they look on the weapon that kills them as somehow unconnected with the soldier who fires it. Under conditions other than these of war, possibly they would be a kindly and naive people. . . ."

"Yeah, you put that down, Gutless Won—" the exhaustion-hoarse voice of Joby broke off on a slight note of embarrassment, similar to that of a person who finds himself talking out of turn and too loudly at a funeral. "—Contacts Officer," he amended.

From behind, along the slope, there was the rattle of displaced gravel.

"Section?" It was the young voice of the soldier Cal had called Tack.

"Well?" said Cal.

"No orders."

There was a moment of total silence. Even Contacts Officer Lieutenant Harry Runyon paused in the dictation of his delirium-born reports to his superiors.

"How about the other thing?" said Cal. "They get the word passed on to Medics we've got a basket case here?"

"Sure, Sec. But they said no beamed-power equipment to be used for fear of the Lehaunan blowing it up. Period. Including ambulances."

The rest of them could hear Joby spit, in the darkness.

"Thought you didn't like Contacts Officers, Joby?" jeered Tack.

"And your sister," said Joby. "He's attached to our outfit."

"Cut it," said Cal.

His own words came to his ears sounding unreally quiet and distant. He was a little surprised to hear them. It was like somebody else talking. The feeling was part of the general sensation he had of being somehow without a body; a feeling he knew was essentially light-headedness from lack of sleep. He had not slept for one —two days now. Not since Lieutenant James, the last combat commissioned officer had been taken off by ambulance, leaving Cal, a Section Leader only, in command of the Wing. (Runyon, of course, being a Contacts Officer and forbidden to take any part in the fighting, did not count.)

"Tack," said Cal. "Up top and take a look."

The sound of a quiet slither went away up the slope from them.

"Truce was up at sunset," said Joby. The Contacts Officer had fallen silent again. Perhaps he was mercifully dead. Neither Cal nor Joby moved to find out.

"Get Walk over here," said Cal. Joby went off, back toward the eighty-three men and the cable phone. Left for a moment with no one to know what he did, Cal felt a sudden, almost drunken desire to lie down. He fought it away from him. He heard Joby's return; and Joby spoke.

"Here we are."

"What's up, Cal?"

The second voice, that of Section Leader Walker Lee Blye, had a quality and tone something like Cal's, the latter's exhaustion-tricked and unreal sense of hearing noted. It was not the same voice in an ordinary sense, being deeper, harsher, and more clipped. But there was something in the phrasing, in the breathing, that made it seem like his own voice speaking back to him out of the pain and darkness of the night. It was as if that part of Cal himself which, suffering, struck out in blind retaliation at the universe, had answered back. Cal pushed the lightheaded fancy from himself.

"Tell you as soon as Tack gets back down here," he said. They rested together in the darkness, the three of them, able-bodied soldiers. Harry Runyon had taken up his muttering once more, but now in too low a tone to be understood. Joby spoke.

"You ever get the urge?"

They thought about it for a moment in the dark.

"You mean Earth?" said Walk's voice. "Stay back there? Go civilian?"

"Yeah," said Joby.

"I thought of it," said Walk. "I thought of it. At the end of every expedition I think of it. But I'm not built for it. When I get rich and they shovel me under there'll be the slow drums and the trumpets. Not some damn civilian organ in a mortuary."

Cal listened without saying anything.

"Lanson went back," said Joby. "No new coat of varnish for him this trip, he said."

"I know."

"He's a Congressman from South McMurdo now."

"Kerr went into business back there. Deep-sea farming off Brazil someplace. Guess he did all right."

"Nah," said Joby. "He got himself another coat. Hundred twenty-seventh Armor Assault Group. Section in Ballistics told me."

"Well. And he likes it. I got a letter . . ."

"After a while, I guess—"

"—we must," said Runyon, strongly and suddenly out of his muttering, "distinguish. The one from the other. The innocent from the guilty. The defenders from the attackers. The—dear sir, if you will refer to my previous reports . . ." he trailed off back into mumbling.

"Lots like him back home now,"- said Walk. Cal woke a little out of his lightheadedness at the statement, and looked in Walk's direction. He could not see the other man, but he could imagine the sudden flash of the white teeth in Walk's lean face as he said it, and the sudden glittering glance thrown through the obscurity at Cal.

"You mean, Runyon?" said Joby.

"Him."

"Don't know why the ex-Service people in Government don't put a stop to that," said Joby. "All the good men and women we lost against the Griella. Now against the Lehaunan. And now they start letting these Societics, these Equal-Vote, Non-Violence people put on uniforms right beside us and turn right around after peace is signed and do their best to give back everything we took. Who'n hell has to make friends with Aliens, anyway? We can lick'm, can't we?"

"Civilians!" said Walk.

"We've got ex-mulebrains in Government," said Joby. "What's wrong with them?"

"Well, I tell you," said Walk, and again Cal imagined the flash of teeth, the glitter of eyes in his direction. "They marry civilians; they've got civilian relatives. It affects their point of view."

"No," Cal made himself say with a heavy effort. "The ones who crack their varnish and quit always were half-civilian anyway. That's what it is."

"Someday," said Walk, "a bunch of us'll go back. Up ship, a full Expedition and go back armed."

"And fight Headquarters," said Joby.

"Headquarters'd be on our side."

"Then why don't they order us back?" asked Joby. "What the hell—you, me, any of us—we go back there and what happens?"

". . . only young men should fight wars," said the voice of Runyon, suddenly and clearly out of the blackness, "to reduce the tax burden and . . ."

"I mean," said Joby, raising his voice above the sound of Runyon's, "I go back. All right, I've got my own vote plus one extra for being a veteran. I got veteran's bonus points for government job tests. I got land option and combat pension. Why fight? I ought just be able to take over."

There was another moment of silence during which Runyon muttered about nothing being more certain than a soldier's Death Benefits.

"No," said Joby heavily, after a moment. "I guess not. Not worth it. We can sweat these holier-than-thou gutless wonders out, I guess."

"No," said Walk. "You were closer to right to start with. You and I know what the answer is—the same answer that always works. Clean them out. Get rid of them."

A sound of slithering descent approached them down the slope, invisibly.

"Sec?"

"Here," said Cal.

"Well," said Tack's voice, now in their midst, "it's still going on. I sat up there with Djarali and watched one myself. Something like a truck, and one comes out of that hole in the hill into that walled compound, up at the far end of town. One about every twelve minutes. Djar says he's counted nine more since he went on sentry; and he hasn't seen any go back into the hill."

"And the truce quit at sunset," said Joby.

Cal stood up. He looked back through the darkness to where the eighty-three men waited. In his mind's eye he saw the heavy equipment and weapons back there all parked and idle with the protection of a little rise in ground between the men and them.

"Walk," he said, "go back and get on that cable

phone. Tell them I'm asking for orders—from the General if necessary. And tell them if they can't get an ambulance up here, they can at least get a runner in here with some drugs for Runyon. Joby can't keep on gigging him with a nerve pinch forever. Tacky!"

"Right here, Cal."

"Got your sketch pad and junk with you?"

"I got a pocket kit."

"All right. Keep that." Cal began to unclip his weapons harness. "Get out of your other gear. You and I are going for a stroll, down into that town."

"Down among those Lehaunan?" said Walk.

"That's right. You're in charge until I get back. I'm going to try and find out what those trucks, or whatever they are, are bringing in. Ready, Tack?"

There were a few final clinks from Tack's direction, and then the sound of a dropped harness.

"All ready. But, oh Section Leader, sir"—Tack's voice scaled up in bad mimicry of a high-voiced recruit—"isn't this one of those volunteer missions?"

"Shut up," said Cal. "You're to stick close and not play any games. Walk, give us three hours to get back. After that, it's all yours."

"Right. *Have fun!*"

"Oh, we'll have a ball."

Cal led the way off the slope, hearing Tack close behind him.

Chapter Two

In the Lehaunan town, once Cal and Tack got into it, there was plenty of light. It came from tall glowing, barber pole affairs that were the local equivalent, evidently, of street lights. They cast a dim but, to human eyes, garish glare over the rounded buildings and small protuberances that looked like half-barrels sticking up out of the pavement between the buildings. Cal took his way from sight-to-sight.

There were no true streets, but simply spaces between the buildings and he had not dared to bring even so simple a mechanical device as a compass, after the way the Lehaunan had reacted to Runyon's voice recorder, some hours previously. Cal was fairly sure he was proceeding as directly as was possible through the town to the walled compound against the hillside beyond, but it was slow going and after fifteen minutes or so of threading his way between the buildings, he sat down on one of the half-barrels and waited for Tack to catch up.

There were two barber pole street lights in this particular open space. One was about fifteen feet high and three feet in diameter, the other about eight feet high and two feet wide. Both glowed with the crackling, hard, amber illumination. It hurt the eyes to look directly at them, but for all their size, the light they threw on the curved walls of the buildings thirty and fifty feet away from them was little more than a camp-fire in the center of the same area would have pro-vided. A couple of the adult, sooty-furred Lehaunans passed in opposite directions through the space while Cal sat resting. But neither gave him more than a casual glance that seemed to at once recognize his lack of a weapon harness.

What was delaying Tack was a young Lehaunan, looking like a black-furred raccoon about three feet high, who had apparently become fascinated by Tack's sketch book and pencil and was tagging inquisitively after the soldier. In the weird glare from the barber poles, they made a humorous-looking pair: the young Lehaunan like a human child encased in animal Hal-loween costume and shoving close to the fresh-faced young man in the dirty coveralls. Tack had let himself be worked upon to the point where he was actually drawing pictures for his small pursuer.

"Hurry it up," said Cal numbly.

"Be right with you, Sec," said Tack. He made a few steps toward where Cal was sitting, then paused to add several more lines to the sketch he was making at a rough distance of six inches under the curious orange nose of his companion. "He's cute. Y'know?"

"I know," said Cal under his breath. He had started thinking again, however, about Walk Blye, and his mind swung off at a tangent. There was a danger in Walk.

The man had a streak in him. Walk was like a wolf the Wing had once raised from a cub and tried to keep for a mascot, until it went berserk in its fifth year and had to be hunted down with fire rifles, out in the boon-docks back of camp. The wolf had been perfectly like a dog in all respects but one. He would press against your knees, shoving his head forward as you petted him. And then, suddenly, there would be something

like a light touch against the back of your hand. All at
once, blood would bead up along a thin line where he
had slashed you. But when you looked from the hand
back to him, there he was, still pressing against your
knees and begging to be petted.

At the end he had gone wild, slashing and butcher-
ing at all things about him for no reason. And when he
had been knocked off his feet with fire rifles and Cal,
who was closest, had come up to do the unhappy job
of finishing him off, he had whined and raised his head
and licked out his tongue at Cal's hand, not as if sup-
plicating or in shame, but almost as if feverishly seek-
ing petting for what he had done. And a hand to slash.

With Walk, the slash was always in words.

"Right," he had said, as Cal and Tack were leaving.
"Have fun."

Cal had been twenty feet up the slope before it regis-
tered on him that the last two words had not been said
in the usual tone of rough and friendly irony, but on a
driving note of bitter, sneering contempt. As if Cal, instead of taking on a risky mission required by duty,
had been dodging out to avoid some unpleasant task
where he was. Like the wolf, Walk had slashed without
warning; and Cal knew this to be a sign that something was eating at the man. The bitter part was that he
was also Cal's oldest friend. They had entered the Service together. They had saved each other's lives before
this, and might well again.

Cal looked up impatiently. Tack and the young Lehaunan were still twenty feet from him, still immersed
in their drawing. Cal got heavily to his feet and stalked
over to them.

". . . a bunny rabbit. See?" Tack was pointing at a
sketch he had drawn and put in the young Lehaunan's
hand. "See the ears? Bunny rabbit. Say *bunny rabbit.*"

"Burr . . ." said the young Lehaunan. "Burra . . . brrran—"

"All right," said Cal. "That's enough." He cast a quick glance around, but there were no adult Lehaunan in sight. "Out!" He took two more steps forward and cuffed the young Lehaunan sharply. "Get out of here!"

The young youngster cried out, and fell back a few steps, still clutching the sheet of paper with the drawing. He whimpered and looked at Tack.

"Sec!" said Tack.

"Shut up!" Cal said. He took another step toward the young Lehaunan, who hesitated, then held out the paper shyly toward him.

"Burraba . . ." said the little Lehaunan, uncertainly.

"Get!" barked Cal, striding forward. The young Lehaunan cried out and scuttled away into the further dimness beyond two of the houses.

Cal looked around, sweating. But there were still no adults in view. He let out a relieved breath. He had been dull-witted with exhaustion a moment before, but now he felt as if he had just taken some powerful stimulant. He was once more conscious that he was a soldier, with authority and responsibility. He was wide awake. He turned around and led off once more.

Tack followed. Cal could feel the younger soldier's resentment like a hand laid against Cal's back.

"Listen to me," Cal said, without slowing down or turning his head. "You're carrying that sketch book to put down military information about this town. Not to play games with. And just because the Lehaunan let us walk around here as long as we aren't carrying any power equipment doesn't mean they're harmless. You saw what happened to Runyon when he went up to one of the adults just wearing a recorder—and the truce was still on then, too." Cal paused. There was no answer from behind him. "Do you hear me?"

"I hear you," said Tack, behind him.

"All right." They walked on. "And if you're wound up because I had to slap that kid back there, just remember that good military practice—the *smart* thing to do—would have been to chop him over the ear and hide his body some place safe so he couldn't go tell the wrong parties about what we're doing here."

Tack said something Cal could not catch.

"What's that?"

"I said," muttered Tack, "I could have chased him off without hitting him, if you'd told me."

"I shouldn't have had to tell you."

They went on. After about five more minutes, they came to a wall of the compound where the trucks had been spotted. They walked along the outside of the wall from end to end. But there was no way to get over, or even see over it, without equipment they had not dared bring. And there was no way visible through it but a pair of blank, high, locked gates. Tack made a number of sketches, but in the end they were forced to turn away without learning anything that explained the trucks.

"We could try up around the hill from behind," said Tack.

"No time," said Cal. He looked at the timepiece set in his wrist scope. "Five hours to dawn. Come on back to camp."

On their way once more through the town, they did not see the little Lehaunan again.

"Sec?" said Joby's voice as Cal and Tack came down the slope near the cable phone and the waiting men.

"Joby?" said Cal. "How come you're still here?" Runyon get rich?"

"No, he's still alive. A tech-nurse made it in from Division on her own two feet. You know that Lieutenant Anita Warroad that came out with the replacements last month? That little brunette?"

"No," said Cal. "She bring drugs?"

"Yeah. She's got him back knowing where he is."

"Any news from Division?"

"That's what I've been going to tell you," said Joby. "There was a directive to all units from General Harmon, over the cable phone. All unit commanders, pending further orders, are to take whatever independent action they consider individually necessary to hold their present positions."

"Yeah," said Cal softly, under his breath.

He stood for a second.

"All right," he said, raising his voice. "Everybody in here where I can talk to them. Get them in, Joby. Where's Walk?"

"Here," answered Walk's voice, so close at hand it was startling.

"Want to talk to you."

Cal led off into the darkness. He could hear Walk following. After a dozen steps he turned and stopped. Walk's steps stopped.

"That order," said Cal in a low voice. "It leaves it up to me."

"It does that," said Walk, without expression in his voice.

Cal waited a moment, but there was silence.

"Have *you* got something in mind?" said Cal.

"It's your show."

"Yes," said Cal. "That's right, I guess. It's my show. All right." He stepped around where Walk would be and headed back. He heard Walk's footsteps start and followed behind him again like a mockery. Cal counted off the dozen steps back and stopped.

"Joby?" he said.

"They're all here," said Joby.

"All right. Section units," said Cal. "Sound off. One?"

"Here," said a voice out of the night, "All present and accounted for."

"Two?"

"Here."

"Three?"

"All here."

He went on down the list of Sections. All six from A to F were there. Eighty-three sound men, plus Tack, Joby and Walk waiting on his words in the darkness.

"Morituri te salutant!" he heard his dead father's voice say suddenly and clearly upon the waiting air. *"Ave, Caesar."* With a sudden superstitious horror he clamped his jaw shut and discovered it had been himself that was speaking with the exact pure accent and intonation of the older man. For a moment he stood numb and shaken, expecting anything in the way of response and questions from the armed and waiting men before him. But no sound came back; no voice queried. The exhaustion-hazed world settled back toward sanity around him. Perhaps, he thought, there was no one among them who had recognized the ancient salute of the Roman gladiators in its original Latin. *"Those who are about to die. . . ."* He shoved the thought from him with almost a physical use of muscle. He cleared his throat.

"Right, then," he said, clearing his throat again. He spoke a little louder. "You all know how we stand. The truce was up at sunset, according to Division. At dawn, the Lehaunan in that town down there will probably be hitting us, especially since they seem to be getting reinforcements or supplies from somewhere underground into that walled power center compound back of town. If we wait until dawn, they've got us. If we hit them now, considering that they don't like to fight at night, maybe it'll be the other way around."

He paused. There was no sound from them.

"So that's what we're going to do," he went on. "Hit

them now. Harness up with hand weapons, fire rifles, only. In five minutes we're moving out in skirmish order of Sections. We'll move in skirmish order right to the edge of the town and when I signal, we go in shooting and fight our way through town and into that compound. That's all. Section Leaders here to me."

The leaders of the Sections—in some cases they were not even Squadmen, so reduced was the Wing's rank and strength—gathered about Cal for their individual orders. As soon as he had disposed of them, Cal went in search of the tech-nurse who had walked in to take care of Runyon. He found her with Runyon in the same anonymous patch of darkness where he had left the wounded Contacts Officer earlier.

"Nurse?" he said, peering into the obscurity. "Lieutenant?"

"We're over here, Section Leader," said a young woman's voice that had some ring of familiarity to Cal's ears.

"You know me? Have I met you before, Lieutenant?" said Cal.

"You came into Medical HQ about your ambulance liaison last week," was the answer. Cal nodded to himself. He remembered her now. An almost tiny little girl with penetrating brown eyes. There had been a shift in ambulance assignments in the field units and she had seen to it that he was put in touch with his new driver.

"I remember," he said. "Lieutenant, we're moving up. All of us. You'll be left here alone with the Contacts Officer. I can't even spare you a man for the cable phone. But if you sit tight right here, you'll be okay. Division'll have an ambulance out at dawn."

"Cal . . ." it was Runyon's voice, weak, but no longer irrational. "You aren't going to attack that town."

"If you'd like, Nurse, we can move you and Lieutenant Runyon back to the cable phone."

"Cal," said Runyon. "Cal, listen. They don't think

the way we do, these Lehaunan. Not like us. I'm positive they think the truce is good until tomorrow, dawn. Don't you see what that means, then, if you hit them tonight? It'll be proof to them that we make truces and—"

"Sorry," said Cal. "But the outfit is a sitting duck for any sort of morning attack from that town, Lieutenant. Now, Nurse—"

"You can't do this!" cried Runyon feebly. "It's murder."

"What do you know about it, Gutless Wonder!" exploded Cal suddenly, as a white flare seemed to burst suddenly in his brain. "You got a theory for the situation? Well, stuff your theory! Stuff your ethics! Chew on them and use them instead of a backbone, you—"

"Section Leader!" Cal found himself literally being wrestled back by the small invisible figure of the technurse. "This man is badly wounded! And he's officer rank. And you can't—"

"And I'm in command here!" Cal jerked roughly back out of her grasp. "Remember that. Both of you. It's a combat area, my Wing, and my responsibility. So do what I tell you and save your breath for the brass back at Headquarters!"

He turned and stalked off.

"Cal!" It was Runyon's voice behind him, calling. "Cal!"

"Walk?" said Cal, halting where he judged the men to be lined up. "Section Leaders?"

"Here," answered Walk. And the Section Leaders also answered. Over their close, low-pitched voices, he could hear the distant calling of Runyon, struggling against the nurse's attempts to quiet him.

"All right. Moving out." Cal led off up the slope into the darkness and toward the distant, sky-reflected glow of the town.

And it was then that his later memory began to fail him.

What happened came back to him afterwards as a series of disconnected incidents, like a badly edited film:

They were spread out in a skirmish line and going down the slope on the far side of the hill. The night-time city was distant, small and amber-colored before them. The slope was steep and he could hear men losing their footing with the weight of their equipment and the fact that they could not see where their feet were stepping. He could hear them sliding on down through the gravel and weeds for some distance before they could dig in their heels and elbows to stop.

"Keep close! Keep them together, Sections!" Cal kept calling.

And one desperate voice finally snarled back, "How can I keep the sonsabitching sonsabitches close when I can't even keep my own sonsabitching self in line?"

A near-hysterical howl of laughter burst out suddenly at this, off to Cal's right. And then it was cut off again, as suddenly as if the laughter had without warning felt cold hands close about his throat.

They were spread out still in a skirmish line, moving up through the level ground of cultivated fields to the town's outer ring of illumination, and waiting for Cal to blow the whistle that would signal their attack.

"Cal?" It was Walk's voice, suddenly and eerily out of the night almost beside Cal's ear.

"What? What're you doing up here? You've got the rear to take care of!" hissed Cal.

"Yeah. And I'm going back there in just a minute," said Walk. "I just wondered if we still had you ahead of us up here, that's all."

Cal felt a sick, hot rage rising in his throat. He took a slow breath and spoke carefully.

"Get back to your position."

Walk laughed, and his laugh faded away, going away, behind Cal. Cal walked on at a normal pace. When he was a dozen feet from the outer ring of town lights, he put the whistle to his lips, and blew.

Yelling and running, the human soldiers, looking clumsy and unnatural in their harnesses and equipment, burst forward into the glare, black against the hard amber illumination, dodging between the dome-roofed buildings, the fire rifles spitting little pale ghosts of flames from the pinholes of their muzzles, making small, dry noises like the breaking of sticks.

Cal found himself yelling, too . . . running, and his rifle was spitting in his hand.

It had all taken on the air of a carnival, of a pigeon shoot. There was hardly a sputter of opposition. The humans were running between the buildings, calling out to each other. Keeping score. Making bets.

Black-furred bodies lay between the buildings. Half in and half out of triangular doorways. The barber pole lights had holes shot in them, but continued to shed their usual glow over the scene. The buildings had holes in them.

They were at the gates, the high, solid, locked gates of the compound. They had shot the locking mechanism to ribbons but the gates themselves refused to open. Some of the men were cheering and rocking one of the taller, thinner barber poles. It teetered. It leaned farther, and then fell. Men scattered, cheering.

It bounced as it hit, like a great rubber toy. It came down again, knocking over a soldier who had not dodged fast enough. It rolled off one of his legs, leaving it oddly angled below his knee.

The men howled with laughter. Joby, who was standing over the fallen man, went into a fit of rage.

"Why don't you look where you're standing?" he raved at the soldier with the broken leg. The man, who had been laughing with the rest, stopped suddenly and burst into shamefaced tears. Walk yelled at the others to pick up the pole. Twenty of them grabbed it.

It was light. Cal found himself holding it nearest the front. Holding it like a battering ram, they ran at the gates. The gates shivered and sagged; and the barber pole rebounded so springily they almost dropped it.

"Again!" yelled Cal. They ran at the gates again. They burst them open and spilled into the interior of the compound. Inside there were Lehaunan with hand weapons who immediately began firing at them.

They were past the Lehaunan with the guns. There had only been a handful of them. The humans were swarming over one of the truck-like devices, halted just outside the hole in the hillside. By main strength a cover was torn off the vehicle, revealing inside it a load of jagged rock.

"Ore!" shouted somebody. "Ore cars!"

The men howled like disappointed madmen.

Cal stared.

Under his feet there was a feeling suddenly as if the ground there, and all the universe attached to it, slipped without warning and rocked, and he . . .

. . . He was sitting on one of the protuberances like half-barrels, in one of the open spaces between the rounded, domelike buildings. Dawn was washing a pale yellow-pink light over his surroundings, and a small, cool wind moved about between the buildings and ruffled the black fur of a Lehaunan adult male, fallen about twenty feet off. It moved on to blow through the sooty body hair of an adult female, dimly seen fallen just inside the triangular entrance to one of the buildings beyond.

A young Lehaunan identical with the one he had cuffed yesterday was tugging and murmuring over the still body just inside the entrance. He caught sight of Cal and for a moment his orange nose projected inquisitively beyond the doorway in Cal's direction. Then it was pulled back inside.

Cal sat looking at the wind playing in the fur of the dead one closest to him. He thought of the youngster he had just seen and his fingers twitched about the fire rifle lying across his knees. But that was all. He had the vague notion that he was about to make some important decision, but there was no hurry. He went back to watching the movements caused by the breeze in the fur.

There was a noise close by him. A voice.

He looked slowly around. It was the young Lehaunan from the doorway. Close up, he seemed even more familiar. He was holding a grimy piece of paper out to Cal.

"Burraba. . . ." said the young Lehaunan diffidently.

Cal stared at the scarcely recognizable sketch of a long-eared rabbit on the paper.

"Burr . . . abbut?" said the young Lehaunan.

There was a coolness on Cal's face in the blowing wind. He put his fingers to chin and cheek and they came away wet. He was crying.

"Bunnrrra . . . abbut?" said the young Lehaunan hopefully.

Chapter Three

———◆———

The next thing was that Cal woke to find himself strapped down in a bed in free fall. Above him was the frame and springs of the bed overhead. Through a maze of such tiers of beds with men in them, he saw a white metal ceiling. He was bandaged high on the left leg and there was a bandage also around his body low on the chest. He lay still for some time in this white world, hearing the little sounds of men heavily but not ideally drugged against pain. An orderly came by with a hypo gun.

"Where'm I going?" Cal managed to say huskily, to the orderly.

"HQ Hospital, back on Earth," said the orderly. He had a clean-shaven, uninvolved face. He found Cal's arm under the sheet of the bed and lifted it out into the open.

"How'm I hit?"

"You'll be all right. Leg burn," said the orderly, putting the hypo against Cal's upper arm. "Small scorch on your side." His eyes met Cal's unreadably for a moment. "From a fire rifle, the report says." He pressed the trigger of the hypo gun and Cal, straining to sort out the meaning behind these last words and opening his mouth to ask another question, swam off into unconsciousness.

After this there was a hazy period in which the leg began to hurt seriously. In between shots from hypo guns, Cal was vaguely conscious of arriving back in Headquarters Hospital outside Denver, Earth, and of some kind of an operation on the leg.

There was a short period in which he seemed to be out of his head. Suddenly, with no transition from the hospital, he found himself back in his father's book-store. They were in the semi-private collectors' room, enclosed by shelves full of not microtapes but bound volumes. Cal stood facing his father, seated behind his father's desk. Above the head of the older man was the regency mirror with the gilt frame giving back an image of Cal's seventeen-year-old face. And on the small shelf below it, between the shelves on either side (holding to the left, Spengler; to the right, Churchill) was a small carving of Bellerophon capturing the winged horse Pegasus. The powerfully muscled arm of the young Greek mythological hero was around the proudly arched neck of a great winged creature, forcing it to the earth. The sweeping pinions were spread wide in resistance, the delicately carved head rearing itself to look the conqueror squarely in the face. The strong equine shoulders hunched in unabandoned resistance. Only one front leg, buckling under the strength of the hero, presented its hoof directly toward the viewer in what Cal had always thought was an ugly, crippled fashion.

"Of course you can stop me," Cal heard himself saying, as he had said eight years before. "I'm not eighteen. You can phone down and say I don't have your permission to enlist."

He looked down at his father, seated in the desk chair with the carved armrest, his father's wide shoulders and upper body showing above the surface of the desk, his sinewy forearms laid out upon the desk's slick top. His father's quiet, long-boned face looked back up at him.

"Do you want me to phone them?" his father said.

"You know what I want," said Cal.

"Yes," said Leland Truant, "you want to go out with a club and beat the universe into submission—" He checked himself. "No," he said, "that's unfair. You want to go slaying dragons, that's all." He sighed. "It's not surprising."

"And you—" Cal looked at himself again in the mirror; his face was white—"want me to stay here and go to tea parties with your Societic, don't-hurt-anyone, friends!"

"Now you're being unfair," said his father. "I've never tried to convert you to my way of thinking, deliberately."

"No, that wouldn't be right, would it?" Cal said, talking quickly to keep his voice from cracking. "That wouldn't be the non-violent way. It'd be violence of the intellectual kind."

"Not exactly," said his father.

"What do you mean, not exactly?" Cal's voice cracked after all.

"I mean it simply wouldn't be fair. That's why I've always tried to avoid it with you. A man has too many opportunities to brainwash his own son, unconsciously, without adding a conscious effort to the business." Leland looked up at Cal for a moment. "If you stop to think, you know that's true. All I ever did was try to set you an example. With your mother dead, I didn't trust myself to do anything else."

"But you wanted me to be just like you, didn't you? Didn't you?"

"Of course," said his father. "Anyone with a son hopes—"

"You admit it. You see? You planned—"

"No," said his father. "I only hoped. I still hope—

that when you reach a mature level of judgment you'll find a greater purpose to life than that which involves killing. No matter how justified." He sighed and rubbed his eyes with the inescapable gesture of middle age. "I'll admit I also hoped you'd stay out of the Armed Services and improve your chances of living until you reached that point of mature judgment. But I imagine I was wrong in that. If you believe something, you should follow it."

"You," said Cal savagely, "talk like it was murder. It isn't murder when a soldier kills."

"Isn't it?" said his father. "Never? The killing of a soldier is always justified?"

"Yes!"

"How can you be so sure?" said his father. Cal felt his chin lifting defiantly.

"Because that's what soldiering teaches—responsibility. A responsible being doesn't engage in unjustified killing, in murder. An irresponsible being under our system soon gets weeded out."

Leland Truant shook his head slowly.

"Yes," he said, "I can see how iron-clad and complete that all sounds to you." He rubbed his eyes again. "But I think you'll learn that the human being is more complex than you think now. We're all potential murderers, Cal. Pushed, pulled, stampeded, or maneuvered to the proper point, we can all be brought to where murder is possible to us. And not just accidental murder, but cruel, vicious, even wanton, reasonless murder."

"Words!" cried Cal. "Words, words, words! That's all you ever give me! What would you have done when mom was alive if some scaly lizard of an Alien had come breaking in here trying to kill her?"

"I would have fought, of course," said his father. "I would have grabbed any kind of a weapon I could lay my hands on and done my level best to stop him, to kill him. And if I'd succeeded"—his voice grew a trifle sardonic—"I was a good deal younger when your mother was alive—I would have felt first savagely triumphant, then a little awed at what I'd been able to do against an armed intruder, graduating as time went on to a pleasant sense of superiority and a sneaking desire that other people should recognize it."

"Then what's wrong with what I want to do? What?"

"Nothing," said his father. "You're just young." He sighed. "Besides the fault is mainly mine."

Cal stared at the older man.

"Yours?"

"Yes." Leland nodded at the books around them. "I thought the best way to bring up a boy was to expose him to as much information as possible. I crammed you full of the books that had brought me understanding and tolerance. I forgot that it's natural for a son to seek an opposite point of view from his father. Where I saw the dark tragedy of Malory's *Morte d'Arthur,* you saw the bright clash and bang of Round Table knights unhorsing evil opponents. You swallowed Kipling by the yard. You knew verse after verse of 'The Ballad of the Clamperdown,' and 'The Ballad of East and West.' You missed entirely the deeper messages that he sounded in the music of Piet Lichtenberg, and 'The Half-Ballad of Waterval' slid in one ear and out the other with you."

His father leaned forward in his chair, both hands spread out on the surface of the desk. Cal saw the cords stand out on the backs of those hands.

"I know," said his father. "I know. *Because I did exactly the same thing, when I was your age!* I needed a faith, too. And I went galloping out looking for a banner under which to enlist myself. And that was good. That was the way it ought to be. But then, having committed myself, I made the mistake of setting my conscience aside. I thought that, having committed myself to a good cause, everything I must do would automatically also be good." He gave his son a long look. "There's nothing wrong with soldiering, Cal, as long as you can keep your ideals about it alive. But God help you, my son, the day you murder them."

Cal opened his mouth to speak, but his throat felt choked.

"I don't blame you for being ashamed of me," said his father. "At your age it must be doubly hard to have a parent who not only was convicted and disgraced in his youth for opposing the present veteran-dominated government, but one who is still unrepentant enough to believe in equal voting rights and mankind's duty to search for a better way of getting along with other intelligent races than outkilling them." His father's hands relaxed suddenly. Suddenly they were the hands of an older and tired man. "No, I can't tell you what to do. I wouldn't if I could. We have to each follow what we believe in, even if our beliefs take us different ways."

The room seemed to waver and fog about Cal.

He felt as if he were exploding inwardly. All the pressure of the years swelled up inside him and burst out of his throat in the cruelest words he could find.

"You always hated them, because they wouldn't have you!" he cried. "That's why she was killed. Because of you!"

He looked furiously, pointedly, down at his father's clubbed left foot—projecting from underneath the desk at one side toward Cal—in its special boot, hooflike and ugly. He looked back up to his father's face and saw the older man still sitting looking at him. His father's face had not changed. It looked sadly at him. Cal felt his inner fury break and crumble into pain and despair. He had done his worst. He had cut his deepest. And his father still sat, refusing to admit the wrong he had done.

"Alexander of Macedon," said his father, "and Jesus

of Nazareth both founded empires, Cal. Where are the hosts of the Alexandrians today?"

Cal turned and plunged out of the room, unseeing.

The mists cleared. He was once more in a hospital bed; in a long ward now with a row of beds down each side of the room. Wires reached out from the robot nurse by his bedside and held him with metallic lack of doubt.

"How are you feeling, Section Leader?" asked the canned voice of the device confidentially.

"A'right," muttered Cal.

A white, translucent plastic tube emerged from the body of the device and nudged his lips.

"You're doing just fine, Section Leader," said the voice. "Just fine. Drink this, now."

He lifted his heavy lips apart, fumbling at the tube, and a cool mint-tasting fluid flowed between them and eased his dry throat. He closed his eyes, exhausted by that small effort. Consciousness of the hospital dissolved from around him once more.

. . . Walk had been waiting for him that day he had the argument with his father, outside the Recruitment Office. Cal saw him pacing impatiently as Cal came slowly up. At seventeen, Walk was thin as a honed-down butcher's knife. And under his straight black hair and startlingly black brows his eyes had a glint of wildness that was close to something berserk. He was like a hungry man who does not care for consequences.

"You talk to him?" Walk said as Cal came up. "What'd he say?"

"It's all right," said Cal emptily.

"You're all set then?"

Cal nodded. He made an effort. "How about you?"

Walk laughed.

"I've been set for months, now. The old man's glad to

get rid of me. Almost as glad as *she* is." He was referring to his stepmother, who was ten years older than his
father and dominated him as she had failed to domi-
nate Walk himself. "I'm not even going back home
again. You going back?"

Cal shook his head.

"Then come on," said Walk. "You want to live forever?" And he turned and led the way into the Recruitment Office. . . .

Chapter Four

Cal began to recover and was transferred to a convalescent section. In charge of the convalescent section
was Anita Warroad, the small nurse who had come
with medication for Runyon, the Contacts Officer. Cal
asked after Runyon, and she told him that the other
man had died back at base hospital. He was surprised
to find that she blamed herself for it, that she thought if
she had come faster or arrived sooner, she might have
been able to save Runyon. They found themselves talking like old friends. As the days went by, and Cal grew
stronger, he found himself being attracted by her as a
woman. They could not fraternize in the hospital, since
she was an officer, but then, before he was discharged,
a field commission came through, making Cal a lieutenant.

Walk—also a lieutenant, now—and Joby came visiting the convalescent section. To celebrate both new commissions, they smuggled in a bottle. They had several surreptitious drinks and left the three-quarters full bottle with Cal. That night, after lights out, he started drinking from it by himself. Almost before he knew it, he had finished it. It had been a one-liter bottle of hundred-and-ten-proof whisky. He was very drunk. He lay on his back, holding on to the nightstand beside the bed to stop the room from turning like a shadowy, seasick merry-go-round. After a while the room slowed down and he passed out or went to sleep.

He woke up in the later darkness of four in the morning, dry-mouthed and sweating. He drank all the water in the dispenser on his nightstand, and then lay back. He felt dizzy, sick, and hollow with fear and a sense of his own worthlessness. He lay still, wishing for sleep, but all he could do was lie there, reliving the past. Scene after scene came back into unnaturally sharp focus. He relived the final argument with his father. He went through basic training all over again. He remembered the first flogging he had seen. . . .

The soldier flogged had been a trainee from his own company. The trainee had been seventeen, just as Cal was. The trainee had gotten drunk, for the first time in his life, on his first weekend pass. He had stolen a copter and smashed it up. The military police had got to the scene of the wreck first, and brought him back to the stockade. But the Armed Services refused to surrender him to the civilian authorities. The Combat outfits looked after their own, the trainees were told. The Armed Services made financial reparation, paying for all the damage done. The company was paraded, the trainee given twenty lashes and a dishonorable discharge. The trainee returned to his own home town and another trainee from the same town was able to tell the rest of the company how the discharged boy made out, having the news in letters from home.

The ex-trainee's father was a veteran of the Combat Services, himself. When the boy got there, he found the door of his home locked against him. An aunt and uncle finally took him in. He got a fairly good job in the repair department of his uncle's general store. The other employees, because his uncle was the owner, did not needle him much about what had happened to him. Nevertheless, some three months later, he hanged himself in the basement of his uncle's home. He would have been eighteen in exactly one week.

Cal did not get sick or pass out at the flogging, itself, as some of the other trainees did. Afterwards, however, he lay face down on his cot, staring dry-eyed into the darkness of his pillow. Now that it was over, some of the tougher trainees were beginning to recover and be rather loud-voiced about it. Cal heard them talking, and after a while he heard a voice beside his right ear:

"Hey, Truant! You going to lie there all day?"

"So?" answered the voice of Walk from the cot on the side of Cal's left ear. "There's some regulation against it, Sturm?"

"Well, hell!" said the voice of Sturm uneasily. After seven weeks all the trainees knew Walk, and none of them wanted trouble with him. He was recognized as a wild man. "It's not as if it was his brother got the twenty, or anything."

"No," said Walk. "But he saw his dad get it, when he was only six years old."

"His dad?" said the voice of Sturm. "*He* saw? When'd they let kids—"

"It wasn't on an Armed Services post," said Walk. In the pillow, Cal squeezed his eyes shut desperately. *Don't tell it,* he willed at Walk, passionately. *Let it go!* But Sturm was already asking.

"It wasn't? How come?"

"It was back during the Equal Vote riots. They sent an Armored Wing into our town to put down the rioting. The Reserve Captain in command had dreams of glory or something. He rounded up a batch of the rioters and worked them over to find out who the ringleader in the town was. There wasn't any ringleader, but he finally got the name of the most respected Equal Vote advocate in town. It was Cal's dad."

"Well, hell, if he was one of those—"

"One of those!" sneered Walk. "Old man Truant hadn't stuck his nose out of doors. His wife was expecting and he was standing by to take her to the hospital at any minute. The captain sent a squad of men to arrest Cal's father. He told his wife it wasn't anything, he'd be right back. But from her upstairs window she could see out into the town park. Fifteen minutes later she saw a crowd with the soldiers tying Cal's old man to a whipping post. She sent Cal ahead to tell them to wait, and she tried to get over there herself. But she fell downstairs, had a miscarriage and bled to death. Now, you got something cute to say to Cal?"

There was an uneasy silence.

"Well, cripes!" said the voice of Sturm, finally. "How come the captain had authority to do that to a civilian?"

"He didn't," said Walk's voice. "Seems he got kind of carried away. Old man Truant got a letter of apology from the government and an offer of reparations later on, but by that time his wife was planted and the fifty scars on his back were all healed. Besides, he's got the Societic point of view: make yourself a good example unto all men."

There was a moment of silence that stretched out longer and longer; then the sound of Sturm's bootsteps going away. The talk took up again in the far parts of the room, and after a while mess call sounded and the voices and a clatter of boots moved out, leaving silence behind them. In that silence, Walk's voice spoke, close to Cal's ear.

"You're not the only one that had it not so good. Just remember that."

Then the cot creaked and his boots, too, moved out.

Six weeks later, when they graduated from basic and got their first ten-day leave, Cal and Walk went to a hotel room in New Orleans and lived it up. Cal did not go home then or later. A year and a half after that, just after he shipped out at the beginning of the campaign against the Griella, he got word from a cousin that his father was dead. Cal had never answered any of his father's messages since entering the Services. He messaged back, now, that the family lawyer could take care of everything.

The dawn came finally. After breakfast Cal was told to report to the Examinations Section for his final checkover before being okayed for discharge. He had not expected this until next week, and he expected that his hangover would be noted and questions asked. But he passed through the physical without comment by the examining physicians. He found himself finally in the office of the psychiatrics officer.

"Have a seat, Lieutenant," said the psychiatrics officer, a major who was a short, pleasant-faced man with a brown mustache, not much older than Cal. Cal sat down on the chair facing the officer and at one side of the desk. The chair was cold.

"Let's see now . . ." The officer ran through some papers and wave charts from various testing machines. "How're you feeling, Lieutenant?"

"Fine," said Cal. "My leg isn't even stiff, and you can hardly see where the skin graft goes."

"You had a burn on your side, too?" The officer frowned at the charts.

"Sort of a small scorch. That was healed up long ago."

"Yes. Pretty obviously a fire rifle burn. You don't have any idea how it happened?"

"No, sir," said Cal. "I was pretty much out on my feet from lack of sleep toward the end, there. Things are pretty hazy after we hit the town."

"So I see," said the major, examining one of the wave charts. "There's a good sixteen-hour hole there in your conscious recall up to the time you came to on the hospital ship. And evidently you got burned somewhere during that period. Hmm—" he frowned at the chart. "It wouldn't be a bad idea, Lieutenant, if we went in there with a full exploratory and made sure of the facts for that period. In fact, I'd strongly recommend it."

Cal felt the coolness of the room like a winding sheet about him. Slowly his stomach began to gather itself up in a tight knot, and he felt an empty fear.

"Sir," he said slowly, "do I have to agree to that?"

"No," said the major, looking at him. "Of course not. You're perfectly free to accept or not, just as you wish. But I'd think you'd want the security of knowing you didn't have anything hidden in that period that might cause trouble later." He paused. "We needn't delay your discharge for it. You can go ahead with that and come back for a three-day psych at your convenience."

"I don't think it's worth the trouble, Major."

"Whatever you think, Lieutenant." The psychiatrics officer made some marks on the papers before him, wrote a line or two, and signed the papers. "That's all."

Cal stood up.

"Thank you, sir."

"Don't thank me. My job. Good luck, and enjoy yourself."

"I will, sir." Cal left.

He came back to the convalescent section to find Annie Warroad on duty. She looked at him oddly, and walked away into the section office. He went after her.

"What's the matter?" he said.

She was standing behind her desk. For answer she opened a drawer and showed him the empty, flat, liter bottle of whisky.

"Well, you know the drill," he said. "Report me."

"You know I won't do that," she said, shutting the drawer. "I'll get it out of here. It's just—" She broke off suddenly, biting her underlip angrily. He was surprised to see that she looked close to tears.

"It's that Walk!" she burst out. "He's the weak one. But when you're with him, you—"

She bit her lip again and turned and went out quickly from the office.

"Weak!" he echoed. "Walk weak?" He opened his mouth to laugh at the ridiculousness of it, but found suddenly that there was no laughter in him. The hollow fear and worthless feeling of the night came back on him. He walked out of the office, looking for Annie. She was energetically banging equipment together in the Section laboratory; she turned away from him when she saw him staring in at her.

He went back to his bed and lay down on his back, staring at the white ceiling.

Chapter Five

———◆———

It was a three-day business getting discharged. In the process Annie's upset and his hangover got left behind together. That weekend Annie took a three-day leave and they flew down to Mexico City to paint the town red. But they ended up in the little mountain city of Taxco where the silver and obsidian jewelry comes from, sitting in the mountain sunlight on an open-air terrace through the long mornings with a bottle of wine as an excuse on the table between them, and happily, no great pressure to talk. For the first time that he could remember, a sense of peace seeped into Cal. And he found himself talking more freely to Annie than he had to anyone in his life. Now and then, even, things came to his tongue that surprised even himself. One morning when Annie had voiced the same thought of peace that lay in his own thoughts, he quoted without thinking, and before he could stop himself:

"*So all the ways—*" He checked abruptly. "Nothing," he said to Annie's look of inquiry. "Just some poetry you made me think of." He shook his head. "I don't know why. It doesn't even fit."

But she wanted to hear it, and so, feeling a little foolish, he repeated two lines of "The Last Tournament," from Tennyson's *Idylls of the King:*

"*So all the ways were safe from shore to shore,*

"But in the heart of Arthur pain was Lord."

Repeating them, he frowned, trying to think why these, of all poetry, should intrude on him here, between Expeditions, in the healing morning sunlight of Taxco. Looking up again, he caught Annie looking at him oddly.

"Something the matter?" he asked.

"It's just that I've never seen you do much reading," she said. "Particularly of things like poetry."

He laughed. "That's for people who can't do anything else," he said. "What say we run down to Acapulco later this afternoon for a swim?"

So suddenly the three days were over. Annie went back to Headquarters Hospital, near Denver, and Cal began a four-month period in which he did little but kill time and use up his accumulated back pay. He received a Star Cluster to add to his list of decorations. But rumors of a new Expedition brought him back to Expedition Base Headquarters, outside Denver, in March. He went directly to the Recruitment Office there.

A chinook—a warm, dry wind off the slopes of the surrounding mountains—was blowing down the company street on which he stood and melting the last evidences of a late spring snowfall. The moving air felt cool on hands and face, but the sudden rise in windy temperature was making him uncomfortably warm inside his uniform jacket. The jacket felt strange after all these months of civilian clothing.

Isolated in the western sector of the brilliantly blue sky, the clouds had piled high into a great, toppling, white castle shape. But, as Cal glanced at it, the harrying wind ripped among it and tore it to fragments fleeing over the ramparts of the mountain tops. Cal's head was dull with a slight hangover. He touched his fingertips to the row of medal ribbons on his lapel, and went inside.

The section leader who took his application punched

for Cal's records. When they appeared imaged in the filmholder on his side of the counter, he looked them over carefully.

"I'm sorry, Lieutenant," he said, at last. "But I can't sign you yet."

"Yet?" said Cal.

Looking across the counter, then, he suddenly identified the look he saw in the man's eyes. It was the same look he had noticed on the face of the psychiatrics officer, and before that on the face of the orderly of the hospital ship. He had seen it, he remembered now, on Annie, when he had quoted those two lines of Tennyson to her in Taxco.

Now it looked at him from the polite, strange face of this administrative non-com.

"Can't sign me yet?" said Cal again.

Across the room behind the barrier of the counter, a desk printer began to turn out copies of some manual with a faintly thumping noise, as of something being softly hammered together. The sound echoed in Cal's lightly aching skull.

"I'm sorry, sir. You haven't been through Psychiatric Exploratory."

"That's not required."

"Yes, I know, sir. But in your case here, the releasing Medical Officer seems to have recommended it as a condition for reservice."

"I was discharged on a leg burn," said Cal. "On a leg burn, that's all."

"Yes, sir. I see that. But the MO has discretion about conditions of reservice."

"Look," said Cal—there was a moment of polite, desperate silence between them—"there must have been some mistake made on the original records back at the hospital. Could I see your commanding officer here, for a moment, do you suppose?"

"I'll see, Lieutenant."

The Section Leader left. A few minutes later he came back and led Cal through the barrier to an office and a seat across the desk from a Colonel Haga Alt, whom Cal remembered as General Harmon's aide in the Lehaunan Expedition.

"Sorry to bother you, sir," said Cal.

"I was just waiting for General Harmon to finish some business. We're updating equipment. I've got a few minutes, Lieutenant." Alt was a dark-haired, wiry man in his early forties, a little shorter than Cal. "You were Combat Engineers on Lehaunan?"

"Yes, sir." Cal found his back sensitive to the back of the chair he was sitting in, all the way up. He made an effort to relax. "Fourth Assault Wing."

"I remember. You got a Star Cluster for taking that power center town in the hills. That was a good job."

"Thank you, Colonel. Not really necessary, taking—"

"'Not necessaries' are usually our main job, Lieutenant. An ex-mulebrain like you ought to know that. Cigaret?"

"No thank you, sir," Cal watched Alt light up. "The Section Leader outside there . . ."

"Yes?" Alt took the cigaret out of his mouth, fanned the smoke aside and leaned forward over the filmholder set in his desk. He studied its screen a second. "Yes." He sat back in his chair, which tilted comfortably and creaked in the momentary stillness of the office. "There's no point in pussyfooting around with you, Lieutenant. Your psychiatrics officer in the Discharge Unit evidently thought you had some possible psychological damage that would rule you out for reservice. It's only a guess on his part, of course. Why don't you run over to Medical Headquarters and have them test you and write you a release on this hold?"

"Well," said Cal carefully. Alt leaned back in his chair, watching. His eyes were neither warm nor cold.

Cal was suddenly conscious of the fact that one of his feet, in a heavy uniform boot, was projecting out to one side of the desk where Alt could see it if he looked down. It must look awkward and unnatural out there. Cal pulled it back hastily. His heart began to thump. Alt was still waiting for his answer. The room seemed steamy and blurred.

"Alexander of Macedon—" said Cal.

"What?" said Alt, frowning.

"I'm sorry, sir." Cal got a firm grip on the arms of his chair, down out of sight-level below Alt's desk top. The room cleared to his vision. "I guess I'm not too good at explaining something like this. What I mean is . . . I understand the digging around in a psych exploratory sometimes triggers off a difficulty that might never have come to life."

"One chance in several hundred," said Alt dryly.

"But if such a thing happened, I'd be permanently unfit for service."

"True enough," said Alt. "But if it doesn't—and the odds are all in your favor. The exploratory will either show there's nothing wrong in this blank period of yours on Lehaunan world, or it'll show something the medics can grab while it's fresh and get out. So you end up qualified for reservice either way."

"Yes, sir." Cal took a deep breath. "But would you like to bet your career, Colonel, even at those odds, when you knew yourself it wasn't really necessary?"

"Lieutenant," replied Alt, "I would not. And what's that got to do with the situation."

Cal let out the breath he had taken.

"Nothing, I guess, sir," he said numbly. He waited for Alt to dismiss him. But the other man sat instead for a moment, staring across the desk top at him.

"Hell!" he said at last, and shoved his half-smoked cigaret down the disposal in his desk. "Would you like to tell me your version of why you think that psych-hold is on your record?"

"Yes, sir." Cal looked out the window for a moment and saw the unmoving mountains there. The words came easily from him, as if he had rehearsed them. "I've got an area of amnesia during and following that attack on the town when I was wounded. But by that time I'd been in sole command of the Wing for nearly sixty hours and I hadn't had any sleep for that length of time. The outfit was in an untenable position and under combat pressures. The truth is, I was just out on my feet most of the time. That's why I can't remember."

"I see." Alt looked at him for a short additional moment, then got to his feet. "Wait here a moment, Lieutenant." He went out.

Cal was left alone in the neat, white-lighted office for some ten minutes. At the end of that time, Alt returned, followed by a tall, spare man of Alt's own age, who strode in on Alt's heels as if to the measure of silent drums. Three small gold stars shone on his jacket collar. Cal got to his feet.

"Here he is," said Alt, to the tall man. "Lieutenant" —he turned to Cal—"General Harmon wants to talk to you."

"Thank you, sir." Cal found himself shaking hands. Deep-set gray eyes looked down into Cal's face as they shook.

"You earned that Star Cluster of yours, Lieutenant— Truant, isn't it? The Colonel here tells me you want to get back on with your Wing."

"Yes, General."

Harmon turned and paced across to the nearest wall of the office. He struck a button there and the surface went transparent to reveal a black background on which a design in white appeared.

"Recognize that, Lieutenant?"

"Yes, sir. A space schema. Our territory out towards Orion."

"That's right. You've had some command school."

"Not officer yet, sir. N.C.O."

Harmon raised his eyebrows.

"We give Space-and-Tactics now in N.C.O. school, do we?"

"No, sir, I . . . looked it up on my own once."

"Very good. Well now, look here." Harmon moved a button and a red line leaped from a center point out through the diagram. "What do you make of that?"

Cal studied it for a second.

"The pattern of our advance, sir, in that quadrant. Since the beginning; since World Unification, at the end of the Twentieth Century. And as far as we've gotten with the Lehaunan, now."

"And to within forty light years of the nearest star systems in the Orion Group." Harmon glanced aside and a little down at Cal. "Lieutenant, why do you think we might be interested, say"—his finger indicated one of the Orion stars—"in Bellatrix, here?"

"Well," said Cal, "it's just about next on the list."

"List?"

"Sir?"

"I said," repeated Harmon calmly, "what list? What list are you referring to?"

Cal straightened slightly inside his uniform. A charge of electricity seemed to have gone through the room. He felt keyed-up, almost feverishly alive.

"No list, sir," he said. "I meant, Bellatrix would be the next system we'd encounter in our normal expansion into space."

"And if we didn't go on with our normal expansion?"

Cal looked up in sharp surprise. But Harmon merely stood, patiently waiting.

"We couldn't afford not to, sir," said Cal slowly. "Population pressures, plus natural instincts—We'd be committing racial suicide if we didn't keep on expanding."

"Really, Lieutenant? Why?"

"Why . . ." Cal fumbled for words and phrases he had not needed for a long time. "Halting our natural expansion would leave us . . . with the sort of self-emasculation that ends in racial suicide. We'd outgrow our resources; we'd be sitting ducks for the first more practical minded race that grew in *our* direction."

"True enough," said Harmon. "But I wasn't asking you for what everybody learns in school nowadays." He turned square on to Cal. "What I'm interested in is your own feelings. You've been a mulebrain. You've seen the Griella and the Lehaunan from the wrong end of their guns. What do *you* think?"

"We've got to keep moving," said Cal. He looked up at Harmon and said it again. "We've got to keep moving." He felt suddenly that he was saying too much, but the words came out anyway. "We have to keep winning and being the strongest. Every time somebody tries to appeal to somebody else's better nature, somebody gets hurt. We had a Contacts Officer with our Wing against the Lehaunan. The truce was on, and he went into their lines to talk to them—just talk to them. He carried a recorder . . . and they cut him—they cut him—" Cal's voice suddenly began to thin and hoarsen. He broke it off sharply. "The only safe way is to be on top. Always on top. Then you can make sure nobody gets hurt. You've got to win!"

He stopped. There was a strange small silence for a second in the office and then Alt, glancing aside at the space schema on the wall, whistled two odd little sharp notes and raised his eyebrows.

But Harmon put his hand on Cal's arm.

"You're a good man, Lieutenant," he said. "I wish half as many men again in Government thought the way you do." He let go of Cal's arm. "Let me show you something," he said, turning back to the schema. His finger stabbed out beyond the furthest point of the red line's advance, at a small and brilliant white dot.

"Bellatrix," he said.

He looked back at Cal.

"That's the star where we're going next, Lieutenant. She's got a system with two worlds that we could use. One of them's pretty much available, but the other one's got a race on it called the Paumons. A red-skinned, hairless bunch of bipedal humanoids that're the closest thing to us we've yet run across. They'll be giving us a run for our money and our lives that'll make the Griella and the Lehaunan and all the rest look like members of an old ladies' Sunday sewing circle. We're setting up the Expedition for there, now. I'm going, the Colonel here is going, and your old Wing will be there when we go in." Harmon paused and looked Cal directly in the eyes. "But I'm sorry, Lieutenant— I'm afraid you won't be listed in the table of organization."

He paused. Beyond the open door of the office where the three of them stood, somewhere down the corridor outside, Cal heard a door slam and a man's voice call out to someone on a note of brisk and businesslike urgency.

"I'm sorry," said Harmon.

"Yes, sir," said Cal automatically.

"You see," said Harmon, speaking a little more slowly, "I've no right to risk the men who'd be serving with and under you, by asking the Medical Service to make an exception in your case."

"Yes . . . I see, sir."

"On the other hand . . ." said Harmon. He hit the button below the schema with his fist. The pattern winked out into blank wall once more. Harmon turned back to Cal. "There's that suggestion of mine the Colonel mentioned to you just now."

"Sir?" Cal was hardly listening.

"General Walt Scoby, who heads the Contacts Service, as I imagine you know, is coming along in person on this Paumons expedition. He was asking me the other day if I knew of any ex-mulebrains who might be interested in the Contacts Service." Harmon smiled a little. "He's having a mite of trouble getting men of that sort of experience himself. Of course, your psych-hold applies only to the Combat outfits. If you signed with General Scoby, you'd be coming along to the Paumons with the rest of us, even if only in a non-combatant slot."

"Contacts Service?" Cal lifted his head.

"I know how you feel, Lieutenant. On the other hand, there's a need for men like you, no matter in what capacity." Harmon smiled. "I don't mind telling you, I myself wouldn't mind seeing someone with your experience and attitude high on General Scoby's staff. You might look at it that way: after a fashion you'd still be working for the good of the Combat Units in bridging the gap between the Contacts Service and them." He paused. "Well, it's entirely up to you, Lieutenant. I wouldn't want to talk you into anything you might regret later."

He extended his hand and Cal found himself shaking it.

"And good luck, Lieutenant Truant. Calvin Truant, isn't it?"

"Yes, sir."

"Good luck, Cal."

And then he was striding away from Cal, out of the office.

It was another day that Cal came across the wide, grassy, parklike mall that separated the Recruitment Office and other Combat Services from the converted hospital buildings that housed the ten-year-old Contacts Service.

He had taken two weeks to face the fact that any kind of Service, for him, was better than none at all. And now, as he came across the mall, the grass underfoot was beginning to turn richly green from its brown tint of winter, and the shadow of the flag before the Contacts Office flashed in his eye like the shadow of a stooping hawk as it whipped in the light spring breeze.

He went up the stone steps and inside. Behind the front door, the offices were cluttered and overcrowded, with a fair sprinkling of civilian workers among the uniformed personnel at the desks. Cal found the Information and Directory desk and gave his name to the middle-aged civilian woman working behind it. He had sent in his application in routine fashion the day before, and surprisingly, that same evening, had come word that General Scoby himself would like to talk to him if he had no objection to an appointment at 1400 hours the following day.

Cal had no objection. In fact, it seemed to him to make little difference. He came now to keep the appointment with about the same emotion a man might bring to having his hair cut.

The woman behind the desk kept him waiting only a minute or two and then took him in herself to see General Scoby.

Stepping through the indicated doorway—at the entrance of which she left him—into a sudden glare of sunlight from two tall windows, Cal caught sight simultaneously of an older man at the desk and of a leopard-sized, long-legged feline of a pale, fulvous color. It was black-spotted and wore a light leather harness from which a hoop-shaped leather handle projected stiffly upward at the shoulders. The large cat lay resting in a corner of the room beyond the desk. It raised its head at Cal's entrance, which brought the eyes momentarily in line with Cal's. The yellow, guarding, animal stare caught Cal between one footfall and the next, and in that fraction of a second Cal tensed, then relaxed, and moved on into the office.

"Good reactions," said the man at the desk, lifting his own untidily gray-haired head. "Sit down, Lieutenant."

Seating himself by the desk as the big cat in the corner dropped with boneless gracefulness back into its half-doze against the wall, Cal turned his glance on the man. He saw an aging, slightly overweight three-star general with bushy eyebrows and hair, a pipe in his mouth, and a uniform shirt tieless and open at the throat. Incongruously, the black and white piping of the Ranger Commandos—the Combat Services' crack behind-enemy-lines units—ran along the edge of his shirt epaulets. His voice rasped on what seemed a deliberate and chronic note of exasperation.

He took the pipe from his mouth and pointed with it at the cat in the corner.

"Cheetah," he said. "Named Limpari. My seeing-eye friend."

Cal looked without thinking at the man's eyes, for they were knowing and full of sight.

"Oh, just periodic blackouts." Scoby jerked the pipe-stem toward his bushy head of hair. "I'm a silver-skull. Plate on most of this side. What's your particular purple heart, Lieutenant"—he frowned at the screen of the filmholder on his desk—"Truant. Cal. What kind of disability have you got, Cal?"

"Sir," said Cal, and stopped. He took a careful breath. "Psych-hold," he said shortly.

"Yeah. That's right," muttered Scoby, glancing once more at the filmholder. "I remember—so many things popping at once here." He looked up at Cal. "In fact, I picked up quite a dossier on you. How come you waited for a battlefield commission?"

"Sir?" said Cal woodenly.

"Don't give me the treatment. I've been there and back, too, Lieutenant. You know what I'm asking." He jabbed the pipestem at the film in the filmholder. "You've had seven years. You got a general aptitude rating way to hell and gone up there. You got a top record and two or three of your medals actually mean something. How come you never tried for a commission before the Lehaunan Expedition?"

Cal looked squarely at the other man.

"I guess I didn't want the responsibility, General."

"A mulebrain isn't supposed to think. All he's got to do is obey orders. Is that it?"

"That's right, sir."

"Commissioned officer might sooner or later have to give orders he didn't like. Might be required to do things he didn't agree with?"

"Something like that, General," said Cal. "Maybe."

"But a mulebrain's got no choice, so his conscience doesn't have to bother him? That so? Then how come," said Scoby, tilting far back in his chair, swinging it around to face Cal and putting the pipe back between his teeth, "how come you took the battlefield commission when it came through for you? What changed your mind after all these years?"

Cal shrugged. "I don't know, sir," he said.

"No," said Scoby, his teeth chewing on the bit of his pipe and watching Cal. "No, I guess you don't. Well, I looked up your civilian past, too, here." He shuffled about and found some papers on his desk. "I'd heard of your father, matter of fact. In fact, I was on the review board that checked over the courts-martial of that Reserve Captain that fouled up in your home town during the Riots. Later on I read some of your father's writings on the matter of Equal Representation and other things. Interesting."

"We didn't agree," said Cal monotonously, between lips that were, in spite of himself, stiff.

"I gather that. Well," said Scoby, leaning back in his chair once more, "we might as well get down to cases. I need you. I need a man with Combat Service experience. But more than that, I need one man in particular who's been in the ranks as well as up in officer country. I need a man who can get along with mule-brains as well as regular officers, and double the usual job and take what's handed out to him as well as I can myself." He stopped and leaned forward toward Cal. "He'll need faith and brains and guts—not necessarily in that order. You got at least two of them. Want the job?"

"Sir," said Cal, and he kept his face as still as water on a windless day. His gaze went impersonally past Scoby's shoulder. "Would the General advise me to take the job?"

"Hell, yes!" exploded Scoby. "I invented it, and it saved my soul. It might save yours. That's a hell of a favor I'm doing you, Cal!"

"Yes, sir," said Cal. He hesitated a moment. "I'll be glad to take the job, General."

"Fine," said Scoby. "Fine. You can start out by ripping off those." He pointed.

Cal's hands made a little instinctive move in spite of himself protectively up towards his lieutenant's insignia on his epaulets.

"My tabs, sir?"

"That's right," said Scoby sardonically. "One of the little monkey wrenches thrown in my machinery from time to time happens to be a Government ruling that I can't use rank as an inducement to sign men up. All Contacts Officers, regardless of their qualifications, must be run through the regular training cycle. Guess what that means? You climb back into issue coveralls and go back through Basic all over again."

Cal stared at the older man.

"Basic?" he said.

"Kind of a kick, isn't it, Lieutenant?" said Scoby. "Get you out on the firing range and the obstacle course with all the other wet-eared recruits and teach you how to be a man and a soldier before you go goofing off as a Gutless Wonder. Don't look at me like that. I know there's no sense to it. The Combat Units' General Staff knows there's no sense to it, with a man like yourself. It wasn't shoved into the Regulations to make sense, but to make me trouble. Well, how about it, Cal? You figure you can still square-corner the covers on a bunk? Or do you want to back out?"

There was a faint, sharp glitter in Scoby's eyes.

"No, sir," said Cal.

"Little slow answering there, weren't you?"

"No, sir," said Cal. "I was merely trying to reconcile this regulation with General Harmon telling me he wouldn't mind seeing someone like me on your staff."

"General Harmon," said Scoby. "Well, you're just a little two-bit Lieutenant, Cal; yours not to question why the ways of generals. Or ask generals questions. But next time you're in the library, you might read up on the siege of Troy." He turned back to his desk. "That's all. You can go, Lieutenant. Come see me after you've been through Contacts School."

Cal stood up. Scoby was pulling papers toward himself.

"Troy, General?" he asked.

"All about a horse," grunted Scoby, without looking up. "Good day, Lieutenant."

Cal stared for a second longer, but Scoby seemed to have forgotten the very existence of any visitor. He was wrist-deep in forms and papers, looking like a seedy bookkeeper, behind in his entries. Over in the corner, the cheetah had fallen asleep and slid down the slope of the wall to lie on its side on the floor, legs stiffly outstretched. It looked like some large, stuffed, toy animal.

To Cal, suddenly, the very air in the room seemed stale and artificial.

He turned around and went back to the outer office. The middle-aged woman who had taken him in to Scoby had his papers ready to sign. He signed, and was told to report in five days to be sent out for Basic Training, as a trainee private.

He left the building. As he came down the steps outside, the sun still shone and the wind was still blowing. Only now, under the hawklike shadow of the flag, a pot-bellied Colonel in office pinks was scattering crumbs to a small horde of clamoring sparrows that fought and squabbled, shrieking, over the larger crusts.

Chapter Six

Four days later Cal lay once more on the slight slope of the sand of Hornos Beach at Acapulco, Mexico, watching Annie swimming out beyond the first crest of breakers. It was late in the morning and they had the beach almost to themselves. Also it was shark season, but the dolphin patrol was guarding the shore waters and Annie was packing a stingaree.

Nevertheless, Cal kept his eye out for fins, keeping the dolphin whistle handy. Otherwise, he simply lay and watched Annie. She swam strongly, in a straight line, her white arms flashing against the sun-brilliant blue of the sea, parallel to the beach. *She's got guts,* thought

Cal unexpectedly. *Too much guts for her own good, if trouble comes.* And then he felt that clumsy expression of his feelings about her followed immediately by a sudden terrible stomach-shrinking sense of pain and helplessness and loss. He reached for the dolphin whistle without looking for it, put it to his lips, and blew one long and two short.

One of the dolphins on patrol curved aside and slid of sight under the water to rise a second later beside Annie and nudge her toward the beach. Her arms broke their rhythm; she stopped and looked shoreward. He stood up, waved 'no sharks' and beckoned her in. She turned toward him and her arms began to flash again.

He lay down once more, the sudden emotion he had felt dying within him. After a few moments she came ashore in a flurry of foam, sliding up on the sand. She got to her feet, splashed herself clean of the sand, and then, shaking her short dark hair clear of the bathing cap, came up the slope toward him, smiling. A loneliness so deep as to be almost anger moved in him. *To hell with it,* he thought, *I love you.* He opened his mouth to say it out loud. But she came up to him, and he closed it again without saying anything.

He stood up. Standing, he could see how small she was.

"What?" she said, shaking her hair back, looking up at him.

"Let's go get a drink," he said.

Two mornings later, after tests and outfitting, Cal took a Services transport with four hundred and sixty-eight other recruit-rated enlistees. The transport was an atmosphere rocket with the same sort of body shell that in a commercial flight would have been rated at a maximum of a hundred and fifty passengers. This one, however, locked on an extra motor and filled its interior with two double-rows of gimbal-hung seats on each side of a narrow aisle. Cal managed a seat by one of the small windows and sat there with his view of Stapleton Field, trying to think of Annie and ignore his surroundings. It would be no trouble going through Basic again, he had told himself. Just a matter of keeping his head down and going through the motions. It made no difference one way or another. He was completely neutral, between the Combat and Contact Services. If everyone left him alone, he would leave them alone. If anyone started to step on his toes, he would know how to take care of it.

He had told Annie, frankly, of his own contempt for the Contact Service and its personnel, the night before. "Maybe you'll change your mind?" she said. "It won't be easy working with people if you think that way about them."

"You don't know the Service," he had answered. "It's a job to do and so many different bodies and faces to do it with you."

For a moment she had looked as if she would say something more. But she had not.

And now Cal sat in his narrow seat, staring out the window waiting for lift-time, surrounded by men in new forest-green uniforms. The sound of their conversation and the heat of their bodies enclosed him in a shell of unfamiliarity within which he was content. What did he have to do with graduations, girls, relatives, sports. . . .

"Hey, Dad! *Dad!*"

For a moment Cal did not connect the name with himself. "Dad" was what they had called older men in their middle twenties when he had been in Basic. Then he looked up. A grinning, young, sharp-chinned face was peering down at him from between the two seats ahead and in the tier above him.

"What?" said Cal.

"Got a light?"

The transport was still on the ground. The no-smoking sign was lit in the ceiling overhead. But Cal saw no point in wasting his breath after the decision he had made to remain neutral. His lighter was in a side pocket jammed against the wall. He reached into a breast pocket, extracted a self-striking cigaret, and passed it up.

"Hey, one of the field smokes!" said the sharp-chinned face. "Many thanks, Dad." Face and cigaret withdrew. A few seconds later smoke filtered down between the seats.

A minute after that there were steps approaching down the aisle. They stopped at the tier of the sharp-chinned recruit.

"Got a cigaret, soldier?" said an older voice.

"Sure, Sec," said the voice that had called Cal. "Not field smokes. But here help yourself."

"I will. That all you got?"

"Well—*hey!* What're you doing? That's all I got to last me to the Fort. I thought you only wanted one."

"Don't let it worry you, soldier. As far as you're concerned, you're through smoking for the next three months, until you get out of Basic. And if I were you I wouldn't try bumming from your friends after you get to camp. I'll pass the word along the cadre wires when we get there—maybe your Section Leader can find a little extra something to remind you to believe in signs."

The footsteps went off. Cal tried to go back to his thoughts of Annie.

"That's kind of extreme, isn't it?" said a voice in Cal's right ear. Cal turned to look into the face of the trainee beside him; a good-looking if rather pale-faced, serious, tall young man in his early twenties. "On commercial ships most of those no-smoking signs have been disconnected long ago."

"It's regulations," said Cal, shortly. But the other went on talking.

"You're Contacts Service, like me, aren't you?" he said. "I noticed the color code on the A3 file you're carrying. I'm Harvey Washun."

"Cal Truant," grunted Cal.

"That's one of the things we'll have to watch out for after we become officers, isn't it? Unreal enforcement of regulations like that, just now? There's a responsibility to the fellow man as well as to the alien—to all living things, in fact."

"That's what I heard," said Cal. He pulled his dodge-cap down over his eyes, slouched down in his seat and pretended to go to sleep. He heard a creak from the seat belt (also abandoned on commercial ships of the present day) as his seatmate shifted position embarrassedly. But there was no more talk.

Forty-eight minutes later they took off, and eighty-three minutes after that they sat down at the field attached to Fort Norman Cota, Missouri. There cadre Section Leaders and Squadmen were waiting for them and ran the whole contingent the full distance back to the Combat Engineers Training Center on the Fort's west side, some four miles away.

It was a soft May day in the Ozarks. A puff of cloud here and there in the sky showed above the straight shafts of the poplar and pine and reflected in the puddles they splashed through; puddles scattered here and there in the reddish mud and suddenly blue and pure as fragments of tinted glass. The air smelled warm and heavy and sweet. About him, Cal could hear the grunts and gasps of his fellow-trainees, as they puffed against the prolonged heavy work of the run. Cal was breathing deeply and steadily himself, and it occurred to him suddenly that after these past months of hospital and bumming around he was in no better shape than a lot of them. What made the run more bearable to him was his attitude. He saved his breath for running; his emotions for things over which he had no control. The thought of this made him feel a sudden satisfaction with his decision to stay isolated, neutral and apart.

"Close up! *Close up!*" yelled the cademen, running alongside the stumbling, winded column of men laden with folder-files and dufflebags. "Keep it in line, butterbellies! Shag it!"

Their voices struck off a faint echo in Cal's memory of his own first days in the Service. The wild sweats and alarms mixed with the tremendous excitement of being caught up in something big and vital. It had been hell —but he had been alive. Or so he had told himself all these years. He pushed the tag-end of uncertainty away from him, telling himself that now, for a while, he could be alive again. For a moment, he achieved what he sought: the slow, sweet twinge of a nostalgia lingered for a second in him.

They were passing the barracks area of some trainees already in the second half of Basic. Tanned a full shade darker than the men of this contingent, they were having a scrub-up of their barracks area. Shouts of "You'll be sorreee!" and "Tell'm where to send the body!" floated after them. For some reason, this touched off a slight uncomfortableness in Cal; a touch of shame which punctured his nostalgic mood. He settled down to his running and not thinking.

About a third of the contingent finally pulled up— having made the complete run without falling behind— gasping and heaving like broken-winded horses in front of the white-painted two-story barrack buildings of the training area.

A sharp-faced man of Cal's age, with the diamond of a Wing Section showing on the tabs of his sharply creased and tailored fatigues, came out of a small Unit Office building and stood on the top of its three steps, looking down at them.

"You shouldn't ought to bring them in before lunch," he told the Cadre Section in charge. "These muck-faces always make me sick to my stomach." Suddenly he roared. "Aten-SHUN! What's the matter with you? Can't you stand at attention?"

"Of course not!" said the Charge Section. "They're a bunch from that Denver Recruitment Center."

"Well, keep the suck-apples out of my way," said the Wing Section. "Or I'll send them all off on a run around the mountain. Show them their barracks. And see they don't get them dirty."

Silent, detached, Cal saw the men around him introduced to the white-painted buildings, and felt the wave of their exhausted relief at the sight of the mathematically perfect twin rows of bunks on each floor. He watched their feelings change to exasperation as they were put to making up their assigned bunks, storing their bag and files in foot lockers and bunk hooks. And then exasperation turned to silent fury as they were directed to remove their shoes and outer clothing and carefully scrub and wipe every trace of dirt, dust or disarray their incoming had produced. Finally, he saw it all give way to numb shock as they were told to take their ponchos and mess kits out into the open between the buildings, and there were assigned a six-by-three-foot rectangle of earth apiece for their actual living. Because, as their Section's Section Leader (Section Ortman) put it:

"Those barracks were built for soldiers, not pigs. We leave'm there so you can have the fun of standing official inspection every Saturday morning."

Then he drew a line in the air with the swagger stick he carried under his arm and informed them that this was the magic line, ten feet out from the building, and he didn't want to see any of them crossing it, except on a direct order.

Ortman was small and broad and dark. He wore the

ribbons of the Lehaunan campaign on his parade jacket, and did not smile as he talked.

Cal was thinking of Annie. Consciously thinking of Annie.

Six weeks later—by the time the contingent was ready for Advanced, the second half of Basic Training —the image of Annie had worn thin. So had Cal's memory of his first Basic, seven years before. A new bitterness had taken its place.

For the first time in his years with the Service, that curious alchemy that draws a soldier close to other men in his own outfit—Wing, Section and Squad—had failed him. He was a man apart. To the rest of the trainees (the facts were in his file; they had not taken long to leak out) he was a veteran. To the cadremen over the trainees and himself, he was a freak—neither true recruit, nor true soldier—walled off from them by the wall of military discipline. To the other Contacts Cadets putting in their stint, he was an enigma lacking in the proper ideals and theories.

Washun, his seatmate on the ride to the Fort from Denver, had tried to bridge the gap.

"I've been talking to some of the other cadets in the outfit," he said to Cal one day after chow. "And we'd appreciate it if you'd give us a little talk, sometime, and help us out."

"A talk?" Cal looked up from polishing his mess kit.

"On how to be a soldier," said Washun. Cal gave him a long stare; but the boy was serious.

"Go get shot at," said Cal, and went back to polishing his mess kit. He heard Washun rise and leave him.

Washun was one of those in Cal's squad who did not fit. Unlike Tommy Maleweski, the sharp-faced nineteen-year-old who had bummed the cigaret from Cal on the transport and was now, after six weeks, practically and effectively broken of the habit, Washun was

having it harder rather than easier. Maleweski had
threatened to arise from his poncho swinging the first
time one of the cadremen woke him with a swagger
stick. He had not, and was now a trainee corporal.
Washun had worked hard and conscientiously at
everything while obviously hating it with a fastidious
hatred. But he talked too much about abstract matters
like ethics and responsibility and was too thin-skinned
for his own happiness. The cracks about "gutless wonders" he and other Contacts Cadets—except Cal—
were already beginning to get from the other trainees,
wounded him deeply. Unlike any of the others, he had
already had one fight with a trainee named Liechen
from Section A over the term. He had gone into the
fight swinging hard and conscientiously, and obviously
hating it, and emerged a sort of inconclusive winner.
(This, because Ortman and another Section Leader had
discovered the fighters and made them keep at it until
Liechen dropped, at last, from exhaustion, and could
not be made to stand under his own power any longer.)

As a result of this, however, Washun, after his company punishment with Liechen, had returned to be a
sort of minor hero and leader to the Contacts Cadet
outcasts. Though he refused all responsibility, they
sought him out with their troubles. And this did not
make him popular with Ortman, who thought the situation unhealthy.

"Been holding court again?" he would ask, as they
stood in line for informal inspection—inspection that
is, of their outdoor, or actual barracks area, which was
required to be as tidy as any indoors. Cal, standing
next to Washun, would see out of the corner of his
eye the other man go white, as he invariably did when
attacked.

"Yes, Section!" Washun would reply, staring straight
ahead, suffering, scorning to take refuge in a lie.

"Washun," said Ortman wearily one day, "do you

think you're doing these men a favor? Do you think it's going to *help* them, letting them go on with the habit of having somebody around to kiss the spot and make it well? Well, answer me—no, don't." Ortman sighed wearily. "I'm not up to listening to Societics philosophy this early in the morning. You men!" he shouted, looking up and down the four squad rows of the Section. "Listen to me. This is one damn Section that's going to pretend it's made up of men, even if it's not. From now on if I catch any one of you milk-babies crying on anyone else's shoulder, they both carry double packs on the next night march. And if I see it again, it's triple packs. Get that!"

He turned back to Washun.

"Shine that mess kit!" he snapped. "Can't you get a better fit to your fatigues than that? If you've got too much time on your hands that you've got to listen to belly-achers, let me know. You've got a long ways to go to be a soldier, Washun. And that goes for the rest of you."

He stepped on down the line and found himself in front of Cal. For a moment their eyes met. Cal stared as if at a stone wall, his face unmoving.

Ortman stepped on.

"You, Sterreir, tear up that kit layout and lay it back down right. Jacks, wash those fatigues and re-press them. Maleweski . . ."

That evening, after chow, a delegation of the Contacts Cadets, lacking Washun, cornered Cal as he was leaving the mess hall and drew him aside.

"You've got to do something about it," they told him.

"Me?" Cal stared at them. "What am I supposed to do?"

"Talk to Ortman. He's picking on Washun," said a tall boy with a southern accent and a faint mustache.

"And Washun's doing as well as anybody. That's not right."

"So?" said Cal. "Tell Ortman yourself."

"He won't listen to us. But he likes you."

"Likes me?"

"He never eats you out like the rest. You don't draw the extra duties. He's all right with you because he knows you've been through it before."

"Yeah," said Cal. "And the fact I do things right's got a little bit to do with it, too. For my money, Ortman's doing just fine with Washun and the rest of you."

"Sure," said a small cadet with black hair, bitterly. "You don't want to do anything for us. You like to think you're one of them, buddy-buddy with the cadre."

Cal looked around the group. They stirred uneasily.

"Don't get tough with us, Truant," said the tall boy nervously. "We're not afraid of you."

Cal snorted disgustedly and walked off.

The first half of Basic had been films, lectures, classes, drill and company small weapons training. With the start of the second half they moved into field and survival training; forced marches, night movements, infiltration, tactics problems that turned out to be endurance or escape tests. The Section was melted down from its bloated oversize of nearly three hundred men to merely double the size of a regular seventy-five man Section. The drops-outs went not back to civilian life but to the 'housekeeping' services, such as Supply and Maintenance. Among them went all the Contacts Cadets in Cal's Section except Cal, the tall southern-accented boy with the mustache, and Washun. And with the going of these other Cadets, came a problem.

Now that the complainers had gone, Cal was forced to acknowledge that Ortman was, indeed, bearing down unfairly on Washun. Though it had not started out that way, Ortman was only human. But if he had the weapon of legal authority in his possession, Washun had the weapon of martyred superiority. It had come down to a contest between them.

It was a war of spirit, with each man trying to force the other to admit his way was wrong. And Washun, it now dawned on Cal with gradually increasing shock, was winning. Already he had bent the minds of the other trainees—the other trainees of his own Section, who did not particularly like him—to a feeling that right was on his side. Now he was bending Cal. And one day he would break, if he did not bend, Ortman.

This was all wrong, Cal told himself. Justice lay with Ortman—it *had* to lie with Ortman. Ortman was doing his best every day to instill in his Section the knowledge and attitudes that would enable them to survive and conquer in combat. And Washun, with no more authority than that provided to him by a handful of half-baked, wildly impractical theories, was setting himself up to treat that knowledge and those attitudes as something slightly unclean.

Cal found himself hating Washun. Washun had broken down Cal's protective isolation. Washun was, as Cal's father had been, one of those who, by an irrational insistence on doing good, caused only tragedy and harm. Cal could almost hear Washun quoting, as Cal's father had quoted:

"Societics: a philosophy which states that mankind can continue to exist only by evolution into a condition in which the individual's first responsibility is to a universal code of ethics and only secondarily to the needs of himself as an individual."

Cal found himself impatient for the day when Ortman would finally lose his temper and rack Washun back for good.

It was not long before that happened. They had been run through the infiltration course several times before, crawling on their bellies over the rocky ground under full pack and with solid shell and fire rifle jets screaming by a few feet overhead. But the day came on which they were sent through during an afternoon thunderstorm. The trainees, who had started out griping at the weather conditions, discovered that the suddenly greasy mud produced a skating-rink surface on which it was almost a pleasure to wiggle along. Spirits rose. They started larking about and a trainee named Wackell either raised himself incautiously or a bullet dropped, as sometimes happened. He took a wad of steel from a high-powered explosive rifle through his shoulder and thigh. He began to yell and Washun, who was nearby, went to him.

"All right," said Ortman, when they all stood dripping water and mud once more in Section formation in front of their barracks. "You all heard it; you heard it fifty times. In combat a soldier doesn't stop to pick people up. He keeps going. Have you got anything to say to that, Washun?"

"No, Section," said Washun, staring straight ahead. Ortman had at least broken him of arguing in ranks.

"No, come on," said Ortman. "I'm sure you've got something to say. Let's hear it."

"Simply," said Washun, whitely, staring at the mess hall opposite, "that that is to be my duty—Wing Aidman to some unit during the initial stages of an assault. Everyone knows that. I won't be carrying weapons, I'll be picking men like Wackell up."

"Fine," said Ortman. "You pick them up. You pick them up when the time comes. But right now you're training to be a soldier, not a Contacts Cutie. And you're going to learn a soldier doesn't stop to pick anyone up! Maleweski! Jones! Northwest and southwest corners of the barracks to shag this man! Full equipment and all, Washun. Get going. I'm going to run you around the mountain!"

Washun took one step forward out of ranks, right-faced and began to trot around the barracks. Maleweski took a cut at him with the peeled wand that served the trainee non-coms for swagger sticks, as Washun lumbered past.

"Fall out! Shower, chow—and clean equipment!" barked Ortman at the rest of the section. "And watch that mud in the barracks!"

The orderly ranks disintegrated, as Washun came running heavily around the near side of the barracks. Without looking at him, they poured into the barracks.

Twenty minutes later, cleaned, dressed and chowed, Cal stepped once more out of the mess hall with his fresh-rinsed mess kit in one hand, smoking in the cool sunset air. Across a little space from him, he saw Washun still running around the barracks, although Maleweski and Jones had been relieved by two other trainee non-coms so that they could dress and eat. Washun ran, not fast, weaving only a little; but his eyes were already glazed.

It was not unusual for a man in good condition to run an hour or more around the mountain before he gave out. There was no compulsion upon him to make speed, but merely to keep going. The punishment was not a physical one, but a mental. The barracks were large enough around so that the running man could not become dizzy. But after about a dozen circuits the mind began to lose count of the number of times the same corner had come up. The turning, rocking world out beyond the barracks took on an unreal quality, as if the running man was on a treadmill. It seemed he had run forever and that there was no end ever coming to the running. It was a small, circular hell in which the mind waited for the superbly conditioned body to give up, to quit, to collapse; and the animal-stupid body, sweating under the heavy harness of equipment, gasping for breath, ran on, struggling to prolong its own sufferings in limbo.

Ortman, of course, could stop it at any time. But he probably would not.

Cal watched the running man. He still felt no kindness for Washun and from his point of view there was nothing wrong with running a man around the mountain. What was bothering him, he discovered, was a tricky point rooted in the sense of right and wrong of a professional soldier.

What bothered him was the fact that the punishment was misapplied. Running a man around the mountain was a last resort; and it was like a scrub brush shower for a trainee that refused to stay clean. It was used for a man who was a consistent goof-off and whom nothing else, probably, could save.

But Washun was not a consistent goof-off. Within certain limits he was as good as any other trainee in the Section. And he was not savable, because he was lost already, to the Contacts Service. Nor could his punishment serve the purpose of a good example to the rest of the Section, who did not walk in Washun's ways, in any case.

Ortman, in Cal's eyes, was the Service. In letting himself be forced into going the limit with Washun, without adequate reason, Ortman had acknowledged his inability to conquer the Contacts Cadet. He had lost. And Washun, weaving blindly now as he ran around the unending white walls of the barracks, had won.

"Truant!"

Cal turned sharply. It was Ortman, coming up to him from the direction of the orderly room.

"Get down to the orderly room, on the double," said Ortman. "It's not exactly according to regulations for one of you trainees. But you've got some visitors."

Chapter Seven

The visitors Cal discovered in the orderly room turned out to be young Tack, Joby Loyt, and Walk Blye from his old outfit. Joby and Tack were wearing Section's tabs, and Walk was now in an officer's gray uniform with the cloth insignia of a Warrant. They had all been drinking and Walk was well on his way to being drunk, although only someone familiar with him would have recognized the fact. The alcohol in him showed only in the fact that he moved a little more swiftly, and there was an added glitter to his eyes which a stranger might have put down to sheer liveliness, but which those who knew him took for a danger signal.

"How about it, Sec?" said Walk to the Wing Section in charge of Cal's training unit. The same Wing Section who the first day had threatened them all with what Washun was now enduring on Ortman's order. "Can we take him off for a little?"

Walk, as Warrant, was only about a rank and a half above the Wing Section, an officer in privilege rather than authority. It allowed him to be more familiar with the Wing than a fully commissioned officer might. The Wing reciprocated. He thought for a second.

"He's not supposed to leave the Wing area," he answered. "But there's a gully in those woods across the road there, if you'll have him back before bed check and in good shape."

"Word on it," said Walk. And the four of them left the orderly room and strolled across into the woods.

About fifty yards back, they found the gully behind a screen of yellow poplar. They made themselves comfortable in it. Thin, flat bottles of bourbon appeared; and Cal learned that his old Wing, along with the original Assault Team were moved in over on the other side of the camp for retraining and shakedown.

"Drink up!" said Walk. And Cal drank thirstily, almost angrily. But there was an awkwardness between them that the drink could not burn away; and he could see that Tack and Joby were affected by it as he was. Walk was an enigma. It was impossible to tell how he felt. He sat in the fading twilight of the woods with them, drinking half again as much as anyone else, as they talked about previous Expeditions. He seemed bored.

When he ran out of liquor and went off to get another bottle he had stashed nearby rather than carry into the Wing area, Cal commented on him, a little bitterly.

"You have to talk very hard to get Walk along?" he asked the other two.

"Hey, no," said Tack. "It was Walk's idea. I mean, the rest of us never thought they'd let you loose to talk to us. He set up the whole thing."

Cal shook his head in puzzlement. Walk came back with the other bottle and the light faded swiftly. The sudden-death drinking they were doing straight from the bottle was beginning to take effect on them all. For a moment time faded and it seemed like the old days. Sitting half in shadow in a stony slope of the gully, Walk drank, lowered the bottle, and crooned to himself in a husky voice.

"*—I—ain't—got—no—ma—ma.*" His slightly hoarse tenor floated low upon their ears. "*No woman, no baby—*"

They all joined in automaticlly. It was the Mourn, the Assault Soldier's Mourn, and they had sung it on a hundred drunks before. Half buried among the encroaching shadows they keened their total atonal lament:

> "*—no love.*
> *I ain't got no no one.*
> *Nothing but—the Damnservice!*
>
> *Left my home and I wandered.*
> *Never thought I'd end up like this.*
> *Name on a T.O.[1] listing—*
> *Number in—the Damnservice!*
>
> *I get goofed and lonely,*
> *Thinking of those things that I missed.*
> *Nothing but a Goddam Mulebrain,*
> *Mucked up in—the Damnservice!*
>
> *Gonna get rich[2] next Tuesday.*
> *Wednesday, if the first Drops[3] miss.*
> *Bury me where they don't find me,*
> *To plant me in—the Damnservice!*

The last of the twilight was almost gone as they finished singing. They had all become to each other indistinct darknesses in the deeper darkness. Cal felt the fog of the alcohol thickening in his brain; and remembered his kit, uncleaned back at the barracks. He got heavily and a little unsteadily to his feet.

[1] Table of Organization.
[3] Glider and Shoulder Jet Assaults—Personnel.
[2] Combat Soldiers Death Benefits, paid to the next of kin.

"Got to go," he said, with a slightly unmanageable tongue. "Thanks for everything. See you mules."

"Yeah." It was Tack's voice. "We'll get together, you get done with this Basic junk. You come looking for us, Sec. So long."

"So long, Sec," said Joby's voice.

"Sure," this was Walk's voice, coming low and clear and hard out of blackness. "We'll see you, Gutless Wonder!"

A jarring, icy shock racked suddenly through Cal, checking him as he stood half-turned. He froze, looking back. Above their heads the first pale sky of night was showing dimly through the inky branches of the overhanging trees. But down in the gully where they were, all was steeped in black. Far off, a bird twittered sleepily.

For a moment stark silence hung between them. And then, awkwardly, in a forced manner, Tack began to laugh. And a second later, just as artificially, Joby joined in. A moment later Walk was laughing, too. And then Cal.

But the laughter was not quite genuine, for all that. Cal found his fingers shaking as he fumbled out a cigaret. Ignoring its self-striking end, he scrabbled a chemical lighter from his pocket. Holding cigaret and match, he took a step toward where he knew Walk must be. He stuck the cigarette in his mouth and snapped the lighter.

The flame, springing suddenly into existence, caught Walk's face hanging apparently in midair, his mouth open, his features contorted with laughter. Then the flame winked out.

"Got to go," said Cal. He turned and stumbled up the wall of the gully and back toward the Wing area. He heard the laughter dwindle and die behind him.

He made his way back into his own barracks building. The lights were already out, except in the squadroom where Ortman slept. The door was open, and as he passed Cal saw the Section Leader working on reports at his desk. Ortman raised his head as Cal passed and for a second the two men looked at each other in silence. Then Cal moved on into the dim forest of double-decker bunks in the big room beyond.

Washun's bunk was empty. In the lower bunk beside it, the tall Cadet with the mustache was reading in the dim light escaping from Ortman's open doorway. His eyes came up from his book to fasten balefully upon Cal, as Cal passed to his own lower bunk, farther down the row. The kit still hung uncleaned on the end of the bunk. Cal ignored it. He stripped to his Service shorts and T-shirt and crawled drunkenly under the covers. He closed his eyes and Walk's face, as he had seen it in that moment's illumination of the lighter, came rushing at him.

He had had to see Walk's face in that moment. And he had seen what he had expected. The whatever it was in Walk that must always cause him to try to push things just one step further, had been at operation upon him. Walk had known that if he kept it up, one day he must push too far, must say the unforgivable to Cal. But, like an addict, he had been not able to help himself.

They had been as close as men and soldiers get in service. But they were now openly friends no more. They would have to avoid each other as much as possible, or someday they would be trapped into a situation in which they would have to try to kill each other. Walk had done it. He had done it all on his own, brought it about himself—not because he was drunk, but because of that inner devil of his which drove him to always dare the precipice one inch further.

He had done so, knowing what he was doing. But in

the sudden flare of the lighter when Cal had looked, above the wild and laughing mouth, under the officer's cap canted drunkenly over the wide, tanned brow, Walk's darkly glittering eyes had been crazy with loneliness and grief.

Chapter Eight

———◆———

Three weeks later, Cal graduated from Basic. With Washun and the Contacts Service trainee with the mustache, and some forty others from other training contingents, they were shipped to Contacts School, back in Denver. At Contacts School, they drew officer's gray uniforms with Warrant tabs such as Walk had worn when Cal had last seen him, and were addressed as "Mister" by enlisted men and officers alike. The first day of Contacts School found them seated in the half-moon of seats of a steeply sloped classroom-amphitheater, facing, across a low section of floor, a raised lecture platform that would place their instructor standing behind a high desk and about on a level with the middle row of classroom seats.

A door behind the platform opened, and a small man wearing an officer's uniform with the insignia of a Colonel limped out with some papers in his hand and laid the papers on the desk.

"Ten-SHUN!" yelled someone. The class rose. The Colonel looked out at them, nodded, and went back to his papers. They stood. Apparently he had forgotten to tell them to sit. When his papers were in order he leaned both elbows on the desk and looked out at them. It was then that they became aware that the look on his face was not that of the weary, little, old, retired officer they had imagined him to be.

"I hope," he said, with a sort of quiet relish, "that none of you considered Basic was tough. Because, you see, we're really tough here."

He ran his eye over their ranks.

"Some of you perhaps discovered that the body responds by adapting to the kind of physical training you received in Basic Training," he said. "It becomes harder and more fit to endure. Our job here is going to be to make harder and more enduring a different part of you than your bodies. During the next ten weeks, we will attempt to do our best, while staying mostly within the letter of the military regulations applying to officer ranks, to break your spirits." He paused, slowly opened a slot in the desk, took out a glass of water and sipped from it. He put it back and closed the slot. "From past experience I may tell you that we will succeed with nine out of ten of you. And most of those nine will be made up of those who make the initial mistake of believing we aren't serious about this."

He paused and looked them over again.

"And of course," he said, "while this is going on, you will be studying simultaneously the three training courses required to fit a Contacts Officer for his triple duties. These are"—he held up three fingers as he spoke, one after the other—"Wing and Company aidman during initial assaults and landings; interpreter, translator, and prisoner-of-war administrator, during and immediately following the campaign; and Contacts Administrator with the responsibility of making friends; with the beings whose relatives we have just killed, and whose homes we have just destroyed, and whose pride we have just humbled."

He stopped. He beamed at them in satanically gentle fashion.

"And if you achieve these things and graduate, you will be put to work doing them in actual practice. *And,* if you do them responsibly in actual practice, you will find that those of the conquered who do not despise and hate you will distrust you; that the enlisted man in general will resent you as someone who appears to try to curry favor with non-humans by bribing them with what the enlisted man has just bought from them at the heavy price of his own blood; and the officer ranks in general will regard you as a spy system and hindrance upon them."

He straightened up.

"Under these conditions, it is taken for granted that you will carry on your duties with a high degree of efficiency, ignore all insults and intrigues against you, and while remaining calm, controlled and pleasant at all times, never allow yourself to lose an argument, or close your eyes to a situation that needs your attention. If you do all this successfully—I say, if"—the Colonel paused to beam again at them—"why, we will no doubt find more for you to do the next time."

He shuffled his papers together and picked them up. They had evidently been some sort of prop, for he had not referred to them once.

"That's all, then," he said gently. "That concludes the lecture for this hour. You might all stand there for the rest of the hour and think it over. Those who wish to drop out will find the School Orderly Room open at all hours. For the ten percent of you who will make it through the course"—he stepped back from the desk so that his small figure with the stiff leg stood in view of them all, and raised his handful of papers with a small flourish—"I salute you, Gutless Wonders!"

He turned and went out by the same door, leaving them standing.

It was, Cal discovered, known as hazing. And it had been practiced by many organizations and cultures since time immemorial, and always with the same purpose: to find out if the individual had an inherent resiliency, an ability to take it, which might be required later on. The only difference here was that it was completely nonphysical. But that, Cal began to recognize, was because it took up where Basic had left off. It was, Cal discovered, as the small Colonel with the game leg had said the first day. They were really tough here.

They were tough in all the unfair ways. There was the matter of the ringers.

The second day's lecture in the classroom-amphitheater (they were allowed to sit, this time) the small Colonel informed them, not without some apparent relish, that there were an unstated number of fake Cadets among them. The function of each of these fake Cadets was to pick out one or more of the true Cadets and try every possible means to make him wash out of the course.

"Their job," said the Colonel, "will be to muck you up—" He broke off suddenly, cocking his eye like an interested sparrow at a Cadet in the front row. "Does my language bother you?" the Colonel inquired, and he immediately began to swear at the Cadet in a calm, penetrating voice with every air of enjoyment. The rest of the Class, craning to look at the Cadet, saw him stiffen, and go pale, then red-faced. The Colonel ran down after a minute or so.

"Nor a word from him, either," said the Colonel, turning to the class and beaming. "But then, I didn't expect it. I've just been looking at his personal file. His family, when he was just about seven years old . . ." He commenced reciting in a pleasantly gossiping tone, a

catalogue of perversions, cruelties and disgraces dealing with the Cadet's immediate family, whom the Colonel referred to by their first name. ". . . now his older
sister Myra—"

Suddenly the Cadet was on his feet and screaming
back at the Colonel. The Colonel stopped and leaned
his elbow on the desk in front of him and listened
interestedly until the Cadet, suddenly breaking off,
turned and bolted from the room.

"Well, well," said the Colonel briskly, "there's at
least one gotten rid of for today." He made a mark on
the papers in front of him. As he did so, his eye caught
Cal's, whose seat was in the front row. "Thin-skinned,
wasn't he?" he said confidentially to Cal.

"Sir?" said Cal, keeping his expression perfectly
blank.

"Ah," said the Colonel, winking at the class. "Here's
one of those stone-wall characters. Pays no attention.
Words-can-never-hurt-me type." He smiled slowly.
"Of course he's had practice ignoring the opinions of
others. I've been through his files, too, just as I have
with the rest of you. This man's father was once given
fifty lashes in his town park for getting some young
men of his town in trouble. Isn't that true?" he said to
Cal. And then his voice lashed out suddenly. "Answer
yes or no!"

"Sir—" said Cal.

"Answer yes or no!"

A whiteness, like interior lightning, washed Cal's
mind blind for a second. Then a molten inner anger
came to sustain him.

"Yes, sir," he said, with no change of tone.

"You see?" said the Colonel to the class. "He admits
it. And you can see it doesn't bother him much. If I
were the rest of you, I'd keep a fairly respectable distance from him. He looks to me as if he might have
picked up his father's—ah—tastes." Someone else in the

audience seemed to catch the Colonel's eye. "You don't approve of my instruction methods?" he asked someone over Cal's head. Cal turned to look as a voice answered.

"No, sir."

It was Washun, Cal saw. Washun was as pale as Cal had ever seen him when facing Ortman. But the sound of his voice was as determined.

"Please, suggest an alternative," said the Colonel.

"I haven't an alternative immediately in mind, sir." Washun went even paler. "But someday something better should be worked out."

"That's enough," interrupted the Colonel. "Your objection is what we call an empty protest and has no practical value whatsoever." He picked up a pencil and poised it over one of his sheets of paper on the desk before him. "I'll give you one chance, and one chance only, to withdraw it. Do you withdraw it?"

Washun hesitated for a fractionary moment.

"No, sir," he said with effort. "You asked me, and—"

"That's enough. Stand up," said the Colonel. He made a mark on the paper as Washun rose to his feet. "You have the distinction of having gained the first credit point I've given out in this class. All of you remember that. You are *supposed* to speak out and stick by your guns, whether it does any immediate good or not. However, Mr. Washun, since the exercise of virtue in actual existence usually leads not to an immediate reward, but to additional punishment, you will remain standing for the rest of the hour, as an example to yourself as well as others."

With that he turned his attention away from Washun and began to torture a Cadet in the second row who had a particularly youthful face. By the time the hour was over he had reduced the class roster by two more candidates.

"Not a good day," he informed the class as they rose to march out. "And not bad. So-so."

When he reached the next class, Cal discovered some-one had stolen his notes from the classes of the day before.

There was the matter of living conditions. The candidates were bunked four to a room, with study facilities, and ate in a central mess hall. The food and beds were apparently good. But things went wrong with them; first one thing, and then another. The bedding they drew from the Supply Room turned out to be too short for the bunks. The Section Leader in charge of the Supply Room claimed he had no authority to exchange it for bedding of the proper size. Sometimes a meal would be unaccountably delayed, or badly served. Solid foods were undercooked, liquid ones, which should have been hot, were ice cold.

There was the matter of uncooperative enlisted personnel. The enlisted men connected with the school were studiedly insulting to the candidates. This was bad enough. What was worse was that whenever they could get away with being unhelpful or outright harmful to a Cadet's requirements or record, they did so. Gradually, the candidates came to understand that there was no single right way of getting through the Contacts School. There was only the least possible wrong way.

There was the matter of individual antagonism from the commissioned instructors. It appeared almost as if the moment a candidate began to acquire credit points as Washun had the first day, a competition was instituted among the instructors to see who would be the first to push him to the breaking point. Verbal abuse and mis-scored tests were among the milder weapons employed by the instructors. Cal, with Washun and a half dozen others, was singled out early for this sort of competition.

But Cal, if he did not have the philosophical armor that he saw in Washun, found a deep and native stubbornness in himself that refused to give ground. As he had told himself, sitting in the rocket that had been about to carry him off to Basic Training all over again, he told himself now that it was simply a matter of putting his head down, pushing ahead, and letting them do their damnedest.

So he did. But as the weeks piled up, the pressure got worse and worse, until he began to feel that he would explode after all; that the moment would come when the upper, sensible, directing part of his mind would no longer be able to hold back the emotion boiling beneath. And the night came finally when he knew that the next day would be his last.

Lying on his back in the darkness, staring at the underside of the mattress of the bunk overhead, a grim solution came to him. Quietly, in the dark, he got up, slipped out of the room barefooted, in his shorts and undershirt, and slipped down the hall of their barracks and out onto the small balcony, to the outside metal fire-escape. Six floors below, invisible in the night, was the concrete surface of the area where the Cadets stood their parade formations.

If the worst comes to the worst, he thought, a quiet tumble off the railing here while smoking a cigaret after lights-out would leave them forever lacking a positive knowledge that they had broken him. A savage, angry joy rose in him at the thought. He would not yield. No matter what happened, he could always wait until the end of the day, until night. And the night he could not face another day he would bring his cigarets here after lights-out. . . .

And suddenly, without warning, sanity came washing over him. He woke suddenly to the irrationality of his thoughts. It was as if a stained and distorted window through which he looked out on the world had suddenly been wiped clean so that he saw everything clearly, without distortion and in its proper perspective. The wild thought of suicide as an alternative to submission thinned away and vanished like a mist on the window glass that had made it perfectly opaque before. The pressures the School had been putting on him shrank into the common crowd of pressures that any living would make upon him. Suddenly he saw how helpless such methods were.

Why, he thought with something like wonder, there's nothing they can do to me; there's nothing anyone can do to me. Death was the brittle final ultimate of any weapon; and death shattered pointlessly upon the spirit of anyone who paid out his life in honest coin up to the moment of death. For the first time Cal felt a little of the great strength that moves men of faith, no matter what that faith may be. And for the first time he thought of the millions, that eight per cent of the Earth's adult population, that believed as his father had believed. A touch of awe at what their true power might be touched him. He went soberly back to his bed.

The next day he woke clear-headed. And when he went about the day's classes, he discovered a strange sort of minor miracle had happened. Before, he had pretended that none of the pressures, the words and actions aimed to trip him up, had been able to touch him. All at once, he found that this had actually come to pass. The attacks upon him had become shadow weapons, wielded by shadows. His gaze looked through them to the more important meanings and things in which they had their roots.

Once, filing in line past the glass doors leading to the dining room at a time of day when that room was dark, he caught a glimpse of his shadowy reflection in the dusk-backed glass. He was smiling.

Chapter Nine

At the end of the ten weeks Cal graduated from Contacts School along with Washun and the rest of the predicted ten per cent of the entering class. The rest took their new Lieutenant's tabs off on an eight-day leave. Cal made an appointment to see General Scoby the following day.

The thin, clear sun of September was cutting squarely across the papers on the desk in Scoby's office as Cal stepped into it this second time. The year had turned the part of the planet around Denver into mountain autumn, since they had first met; and the point of that meeting lay many millions of miles back along the Earth's path through that space which is also time. Scoby sat as he had sat before, but the cheetah, Limpari, this time lay alongside the desk, at desk-top level, forelegs stretched out so that the light-colored puffs of her paws rested barely against the sleeve of Scoby's shirt, feline head laid upon those forelegs. Her animal eyes turned to Cal as he entered, but nothing else about her moved. Scoby looked up.

"Well, Lieutenant," he said. "Sit down."

Cal sat.

"You said to come see you, General," he said, "after I got through Contacts School."

"That's right." Scoby reached for his pipe and began

to fill it, considering Cal coolly. "So you got through all right."

Something about the question operated against the relative peace of mind Cal had discovered during the later days at the Contacts School. An old defensiveness came back, an old, sharp edge unsheathed itself in him.

"The General didn't expect me to?"

"Now there," said Scoby, striking a light to his pipe and puffing on it, "is why I want you for the job I have in mind and I'm afraid of you at the same time."

"Sir?"

"You're management training material," said Scoby. "I want you as high up in my organization as you can climb. But I don't want you coming along faster than you're ready to. Tell me about the Paumons. What'd you learn about them at Contacts School?"

Cal frowned.

"Very humanlike," he said. "Human enough to get by in a crowd of us, almost. Stripped, of course, you'd notice differences. But with clothes, they'd look sort of like eskimos with sunburns."

"Ah. . . ." Scoby closed his eyes. "What's the name for them?"

"Sir?"

"The mulebrains and anybody else who knows about them. What're they calling these Paumons people?"

"Oh," said Cal. "Progs."

"Standing for what? What d'you call them?"

"Standing for what?" echoed Cal. "I don't know, sir. Myself, sometimes I call them Progs. Or Paumons. Depends on who I'm talking to."

"Yeah," said Scoby. "You got a ways to go yet. What about their culture."

"Industrial. They get their power from volcanic taps."

"Art? Philosophy?"

Cal stared at the older man.

"Art?" he said slowly. "Philosophy? School didn't give us anything on that."

"And of course you didn't go look it up on your own. What's the job the Contacts Service is supposed to do? Can you tell me that?"

"Yes, sir," answered Cal. "Just as the Armed Services' job is to subdue the enemies of the human race, the Contacts Service's job is to lay a basis for future peaceful co-existence with those former enemies."

"Oh," said Scoby, "but you're a great little quoter, Lieutenant. Now tell me how you're going to do it."

"Establish workable relationships with Paumons leaders and enlist their cooperation in working out future patterns of co-existence."

"Damn you!" shouted Scoby, suddenly, slamming the desk top with one hand. The cheetah's head came up like a striking cobra's. "I didn't ask you for chapter and verse! I asked you what you're going to *do!*"

"My job," said Cal, staring into the other man's eyes. "What I'm told to do."

"And I tell you," snarled Scoby, leaning toward him, "that nobody's going to tell you what to do. You're going to do what you have to do, what you think you ought to do. You're going to have to work it all out for yourself!" He glared at Cal. "You know why there's nothing about philosophy or art in the Paumons course? Because I told them there wasn't to be any. You want to find out about these people, you go find out about them for yourself. Far as the Assault Team's concerned, you're a goddam aidman, and a goddam interpreter and a goddam headache. Far as *I'm* concerned, you're a goddam substitute working Christ and I expect you to produce!"

He sat glaring at Cal for a long second. Cal looked back without moving his head.

"All right," said Scoby more calmly—Limpari put

her head down again. "As I say, I expect something
more of you than I do of what I ordinarily get for help.
I've got a special assignment for you. Contacts Officer
—with your old outfit."

Cal felt a soundless shock. It was something like the
feeling that had followed Walk's last words three
months before.

"Want to back out?" jeered Scoby, staring at him
closely.

"No, sir," said Cal.

"Then take off." Scoby went unceremoniously back to
the papers on his desk. Cal rose and left.

He had been due for a several-week course with the
Medics to fit him for his aidman duties. He had planned
to meet Annie that evening when she came off shift at
the Service Hospital. He had even sourly made up his
mind to get to the library and do some extra-curricular
reading on the Paumons, in line with what Scoby had
said. None of these things took place.

That afternoon, even as he was walking out of
Scoby's office, things were "breaking," as the News Services said, with the Paumons situation. The Cabinet on
Earth was being called into emergency meeting. Six
hours later he was collected by military patrol and
confined to base with all other uniformed personnel on
a general muster order. Seventy-eight hours later, he and
the rest connected with the Paumons Expedition Assault
Force were spaceborne.

Quarters on their ship, as on all ships of the Assault
Force, were close; and all experienced Service people
were on their best behavior with each other. Cal met the
other officers of his Wing. Walk, as the only former
member of the unit, was Section Commander of Section
A of the Wing, and executive officer under Wing Captain Anders Kaluba, who now headed the outfit. Kaluba
was a pleasant, dark-skinned man, who had been a

lieutenant with the Seventy-second Combat Engineers against the Lehaunans. He did not seem unduly prejudiced against Contacts Officers. And Walk, when he met Cal, was almost subdued. He said little. Joby Loyt was Section Leader under Walk. Tack had been promoted to Wing Section for the outfit, and talked and acted older than before.

The Assault Force was on the jump for nine days— and fourteen hours out of destination. An order was posted for an orientation address by General Harmon, the Force Commander, to all officers and men on all ships at X minus 1200 hours. On Cal's ship they took down the hammocks in the main room and everybody crowded in, sitting cross-legged in ranks upon the cold metal flooring. At the far end of the room there was a viewing platform.

At 1200 hours precisely, the platform lit up with a three dimensional representation of the Force Commander's office on the flagship. It showed a desk, a wall representation of the Paumons world, and a door. At a couple of minutes past twelve, the door opened, and the image of Harmon strode out before the audience. He was wearing combat coveralls with a field dress jacket over them and a light-weapons harness with, however, no weapons clipped to it. He nodded into the pickup; a warming current ran through the audience in Cal's ship. Harmon looked slightly tired, but confident.

"I won't keep you," he said. "I want you all to turn in as soon as I'm through and get as much rest as you can."

He picked up a pointer from the desk and turned to the wall representation of the Paumons.

"Here," he said, indicating a squarish-looking continent spreading south and west from the planet's equator, "is the high central plateau area which Intelligence has decided would be the most promising location for our initial drops. The weather is uniformly clear and good at this time of year. The terrain is both highly defensible because of its ruggedness, and adapted to our overland transport. It also overlooks the industrial centers of this key continent. You'll all be getting full details from your individual Commanders."

He laid the pointer aside and came to stand looking out over the desk at them all. There was a moment of silence in the main room of Cal's ship. Across the room, somebody coughed, and a couple of other barks answered from nearby.

"Fort Cota hack," muttered a voice behind Cal. He shifted his haunches on the hard metal plates. Around him the room was filled with the smell of still air heavy with the odors of clothing and other men's bodies. Jump boots squeaked on the flooring and coveralls rustled as those about him fidgeted and shifted.

Harmon cleared his throat.

"The alien enemy we will be facing in a few hours is tough. We might as well face that fact. But, being an alien, the alien is not as tough as we are. The Prog is going to find out that he's bitten off something he can't chew at all."

Harmon clasped his hands behind him and stood out from behind the desk.

"When a human being fights, he knows what he's fighting for. That's one reason we've got it all over the alien, the alien is not as tough as we are. The Prog is different. He doesn't know. All he knows is some other alien got him stirred up, or some sort of alien sacred cow got trampled on, or it just looks like a good opportunity for him to grab something. But it's a human being's right and duty to know what he's about. And so I'm just going to take a minute or two out here, and bring you officers and men up to date on the events that require us to be here."

Cal's underneath foot was going to sleep. He quietly uncrossed his legs, bringing the numb one on top.

"As you all know," Harmon was saying, "ours is an expanding culture and requires us to be continually on the lookout for additional living room. Three years ago, we made contact with the Bellatrix solar system and set down token bases on two of the empty, less habitable planets. At the same time we contacted the Progs to explain we were only interested in what they did not have, and didn't intend to bother them in any way."

"Move, will you!" hissed a man in the row behind Cal and off to his right. "You're crowding my goddam knee."

"Shove your knee!" retorted another whisper. "I haven't got any more room to move than you have."

"However, they withheld official acceptance of our presence in their solar system," Harmon's voice was continuing. "And shortly after that, less than six months ago, presented us with an official complaint against what they termed an offensive build-up of military equipment and personnel in these areas. We attempted to negotiate, but a month ago we were given what amounted to an ultimatum to pull out of the Bellatrix system. Ten days ago, the Prog attacked without warning and took over both our peoples and our property. Twelve hours from now, he's going to have to answer for that to us."

Harmon's glance swept from left to right in front of him.

"That's it, Assault Soldiers. Turn in now and get some rest—and tomorrow we give 'em hell!"

He threw a slight wave of his hand, turned about, strode back through the imaged door, and out. The stage winked blank and bare. The seated men rose, grunting and stretching, and the room was suddenly overcrowded. By orderly masses, they moved back along narrow corridors to their individual unit rooms, where the thick-hung hammocks drooped like white foliage from the low ceilings.

Pushing between the hammocks and the men climbing into them Cal heard his name called by Wing Captain Kaluba. He went toward the corner of the room that was Kaluba's.

Kaluba, because of the necessities imposed by rank and his duties, did not have a hammock, but a cot and a small folding desk. He was sitting on the cot behind the desk as Cal shoved past two filled hammocks to come into view.

"Yes, sir?" said Cal.

Kaluba was stacking reports in a neat pile. He looked up.

"Oh, yes. Lieutenant, you're not to go down with the outfit on the drop. You can come later with the medics."

Cal frowned.

"Sir?" he said. "I'm supposed to be aidman for this Wing."

"I know," said Kaluba. "I've picked a couple of the older men to fill in that duty." There was an awkward pause.

"Can I ask why, Captain?" said Cal.

"I suppose so," said Kaluba. His dark face looked tired. "You're an ex-mulebrain. And it's my commission if you take an active action in combat—you know the regulations. I think it'd be better all around if you weren't in on the drop."

"The Captain," said Cal, "doesn't trust me?"

"I don't trust your reflexes." Kaluba lowered his voice. "Fifteen hours from now, or less, some of these men will be badly hurt, and others will be dying. Are you dead sure you can just stand around and watch that happening?"

"That's right," said Cal.

"Well, I'm not."

"Captain," said Cal, "I think you may have just talked yourself into something. I'm aidman for this outfit, and you're going to need me on this drop." He kept his eyes steadily on Kaluba. "You're going to need every man on the list."

Kaluba chewed his lower lip angrily.

"I'm trained and I'm experienced," said Cal. "You leave me back up here and I'll write a letter of complaint to the Service accusing you of a personal bias against me. I don't think the reviewing board will think your reasons strong enough."

Kaluba's eyes flickered up at him. Then he looked down at the reports and swore.

"All right," he said. "Get some sleep."

Cal went back to his hammock and climbed in. Beside him, Wajeck, the Lieutenant officering B Section, was lying on his back in his hammock, gazing at the ceiling ten inches away. His hairy-backed hands were gripping the edges of his hammock.

"Think of six beautiful women," Cal said to him.

"I'm all right," said Wajeck, not taking his eyes off the ceiling. "I'm just not sleepy."

They made their first wave landing thirteen hours later, the assault glider that carried Cal along with A and B Sections screaming in at five hundred feet of altitude to eject them right and left like tossed popcorn. Cal cut wide on his shoulder jets with a short burst and slid in to earth under a tree so like a terran cottonwood it was hard to tell the difference. The trees on windy hillsides on Lehaunan had been warped and strangely twisted like high-mountain conifers. On the world of the Griella, there had been no true trees. Only a sort of large bush. But here the trees were like trees and the cut-up rocky country all around and between them greened with a heavy moss that almost resembled grass.

Cal jettisoned his jets and checked his wrist scope. All the men of the two sections were down without trouble and already moving in on the red dot which marked the location of the senior Section Commander.

That would be Walk. Cal took a bearing and moved, too.

He was two-thirds of the way to the twenty-foot-high cluster of rock where the red dot showed, when the first Paumons seeker torp came over the small hill at his left. It flashed black for a moment in his vision like a gnat flying right into his eye. And then the rocks he was headed for went up in a graceful, vase-shaped gout of brown earth and debris.

"Spread out! Spread out!" yelled Cal automatically. "Torps."

He had gone down without thinking at the black flicker in his vision. Now he rose and ran, changing direction, for the rocks. When he got there, he found a crater, five dead men, a boy with one leg blown off, and Lieutenant Wajeck. Wajeck was sitting up against a rock, apparently unhurt, but hugging himself as if he were cold.

"You all right?" said Cal to Wajeck. He got no answer. Cal turned to the boy with his leg off and got a shot into him and a tourniquet around the pressure point just inside the midthigh. He set the tourniquet to loosen at fifteen minute intervals—the boy was out cold—and turned to Wajeck.

"What's wrong with you?" he said, and pulled at the folded arms.

"Oh, God," said Wajeck, "I knew it. Right in the middle. I knew it, I knew it."

Cal got the arms apart and there was blood soaking through all over the stomach area of Wajeck's coveralls. There was a slit in the cloth like a torp fragment might make. Cal put his fingers in it, tore it wide, and looked inside. It was a bad hole. He got a patch on it and gave the other man a shot, but Wajeck's face was already beginning to go pinched and strange. Another torp came suddenly over the hills and Cal jerked Wajeck down with him to the ground, as the explosion went off not fifty yards from them.

"Oh, God," said Wajeck, quite plainly and clearly in Cal's ear as they lay on the ground together. "I knew it. I was sure. I knew it."

"Where's Walk?" said Cal. Another torp went off to their right.

"They switched him to Kaluba's glider. Last minute. He didn't come down with us. Oh, God . . ."

"Where're your Section Leaders?"

"There. There. Squadmen, too—" Wajeck twitched a hand and wrist toward the hole the torp had left and the dead bodies in and about it. "I told them to close when we ejected. So we'd come down ready to organize."

Cal stared along six inches of dirt at Wajeck's profile, staring up at the cloudless sky.

"Didn't you learn—" Cal broke off. "Somebody's got to get these men out of here. You must have a noncom somewhere still out there."

"No one. No one," said Wajeck's lips to the sky. They stopped suddenly. Jerkily his head turned sideways. He looked along the ground into Cal's eyes.

"You," he said. "You know what to do. Take over, for God's sake. You got to take over, Cal. Right now."

There was a shriek and a roar. A torp exploded so close to them it brought dirt raining down about them. The boy with the leg off had just come to, and he was hit again. He began screaming.

Chapter Ten

———◆———

The men were dying, and someone was weeping. Looking around under the thunder and ground-shake of the nearby exploding torps, Cal saw the one who wept was the boy with his leg off. He was lying on his back looking at the sky and tears were running out of the corners of his eyes, back into the blond sideburns in front of his ears. Cal looked back at Wajeck, who was trying to get the command scope off his wrist. But his fingers were already too weak to stretch the expansion band over his hand and the scope kept slipping back to his wrist.

"You got to!"

"I can't," said Cal. "Kaluba wasn't going to let me come on this drop because he figured I'd do something like that. It's my orders."

"You gut," said Wajeck, still fumbling like a baby with the expansion band. "You don't care about these men; you only care about keeping your uniform. Nobody lives by orders all the way, you know that." He was still fumbling with the scope band. "I'm going to make you do it, you lousy gut."

"Quit wearing yourself out," said Cal. He pulled the arm with the scope out of Wajeck's weak grasp of the other hand, and lifted arm, scope and all to his lips. He pressed the talk button. "All right, men," he said into it, "this is Lieutenant Truant. Lieutenant Wajeck is out of action, and so are all the non-coms. I'm a Contacts Officer and you know I can't take over. You need somebody in here to take over the command scope. I'll help all I can once one of you gets here. But that's my limit. Those torps'll have us all in another ten minutes, unless one of you forgets all he ever learned about not volunteering. Somebody better make up his mind and get in here fast."

For a moment there were no explosions. In the unusual silence that suddenly seemed all wrong, Cal looked about him. There were two or three large holes in the open space around him, but it looked like very little damage, just by itself. He had to remember that the seeker mechanism on the torps would almost certainly have found at least one man where every hole was now.

An assault soldier dodged out from behind a tree about eighty yards away and began running towards the rocks where Cal lay. Another broke cover off to the left about the same time, but, seeing the first ahead of him, dodged back again.

Cal counted the seconds, watching the man come on. But nothing happened. Only, the second after the man threw himself down beside Cal and Wajeck, a torp flitted over the hilltop and exploded to their left.

The man was in his thirties, small, with a sort of hazelnut-shaped face. Cal searched his memory.

"Mahauni?" he said.

"Yes, sir," said Mahauni. "What do I do?"

"What you think you ought to do," said Cal. "It's your show."

"Yes, sir. What would you do?"

"Get the men on the move. Keep them at least fifty feet apart." Cal pointed at the command scope on Wajeck's wrist. In a larger circle around the unit dots were the battalion signals, clustered now to their west. The two Sections under Wajeck had come down in this little area with a low, open hill to their east, scattered trees and, to the west, rising clusters of trees to a wooded horizon. Beyond that, about eight miles off, was battalion command.

"Perimeter's about five miles," said Cal. "When I was a soldier they had anti-torp defenses along battalion perimeters. I'll take the Lieutenant. You take the kid, there."

"Right," said Mahauni. He moved like an old hand, stripping the command scope off Wajeck's wrist and talking into it. He gave commands as if he might have been a Section Leader once. Or better.

"Ready to move," he said to Cal finally, the command scope now on his own thin, brown wrist.

They moved. The rest of it was simply horribly hard work, running and climbing with a wounded man apiece on their backs, shouting commands at the rest of the two Sections of men, and being lucky when the torps came over. They made it over the hill and safely at last within battalion defenses, with fifty-three men left out of a hundred and eighty-one that had been dropped.

By the evening of the day of the first drops, waves one, two and three of the Initial Assault Team were down on the Paumons ground, and regrouped. They formed a curving, staggered line of battalion fronts, arching around three Paumons cities and several hundred small settlements. The settlements were essentially housing centers, the cities essentially factory complexes for Paumons heavy industry, which here was supplied by power from volcanic taps.

Cal, having checked in with Kaluba, had received permission to leave for a few hours and make contact with his own Contacts Service Command, for instructions. His supplementary and unannounced reason was to tell his story of the drop to someone like Scoby (who was in Contacts Service Command, along on the Expedition) before any other version of it should reach him. He had no idea where C.S. Command Headquarters was so he hunted up Expedition Command, where he would be able to get directions. He found it just a little before sunset—a camouflaged cluster of domes in a little clearing surrounded by tall trees of a cottonwood-like variety.

"Contacts Services HQ?" he asked a Wing Section who was passing between the domes.

"Contacts Services HQ?" he asked a Wing Section who was passing between the domes.

"Check with the liaison desk, Command HQ, Dome Eight," said the Wing Section, brusquely, looking only at the Command Service patch on Cal's breast pocket and not at Cal's face. He pulled away and hurried off.

Cal found Dome Eight. He stepped through the vibration screen at its entrance and found himself in an outer office with several empty desks and chairs. A door in a thin partition led to an inner office from which the sound of a conversation came. It occurred to Cal belatedly that this would be the time for evening chow. The people belonging to the outer office, including the Liaison Desk Officer, would be off eating. He moved toward the inner office, then checked as he recognized one of the conversing voices as General Harmon's, the other as Colonel Alt's. It would hardly do to use the Commanding General of the Expedition and his aide as an information service. Cal took a seat beside the partition to wait for the return of the Liaison Desk Officer.

"—bismuth," Harmon's voice sounded thinly through the partition. "Their communications system depends on those thermopiles. We seal off this manufacturing area and they've got to come to us. Then we can make other drops. Here, hit them here, Zone Five. Zone Three. Around the planet here, in this mountainous section—Zone Eleven. By the way, we'll have to watch that spot for mop-up toward the end, Hag. It's natural country for a regular hornet's-nest of guerrillas. Put a strong-point outside the mountains under somebody fitted for the work. But don't overload him with men. . . ."

Cal dismissed the voices and let his thoughts drift off to the subject of Annie. She would be with the Medics main unit, and that, too, would be locatable through the Liaison Desk. But he would not have time after finding Contacts Service HQ and telling his story. . . .

". . . 4th Assault Wing, 91st Combat Engineers," Alt was saying. Cal came alert with a jerk, hearing his own outfit mentioned. "A couple of sections, I understand."

"Yes," said Harmon's voice. "But outside of a couple of incidents like that, it was a near-perfect drop. Almost too perfect. We've got a fifty-year advantage in weapons on these Paumons, and it's making for too much complacency on our side."

"The men'll stiffen up as they get more action," said Alt.

"No doubt. But will it be soon enough? Soldiers aren't supposed to regard the enemy with good-humored contempt. They're supposed to hate 'em, and have a healthy fear of them. Anything else results in a lot of throats being cut the first dark night."

"I'll write up a general order."

"No good, Hag. Half the trouble's with the Progs. They're treating us as if we're halfway civilized, and we're treating them as if they were. Everybody forgets their fighting force outnumbers ours six hundred to one from a mathematical standpoint. One of these days we'll wake up to find we've half-civilized ourselves into being completely surrounded and defeated." Harmon broke off suddenly. "I've got it."

"Yes?"

"We've got about five hundred prisoners down below Headquarters here, haven't we?"

"That's right, General."

"Pick a town behind our front here—say, this place here. What's its Prog name? Manaha? Get a good, stiff man and have him march those prisoners there, wounded and all. You understand, Hag?"

There was a slight pause. Cal suddenly sat bolt upright, listening.

"I think so, sir," came Alt's voice.

"I'm not going to give any orders. Don't you, either. Just pick the right man."

"Yes, sir. I think I know who I can get."

"Handle that march right, and the word'll get out fast enough. It'll stiffen up the Paumons, and the Paumons'll take care of stiffening up our own boys. That's what—"

Quickly and quietly, Cal got up and out of the dome. He was in the new darkness of early night among the trees surrounding the Headquarters area, headed downhill, before he slowed. The little breeze among the trees felt abruptly cool on his forehead.

He kept going. The business of telling his story of the drop to Contacts HQ would have to wait, now. He stopped abruptly. He had headed off without thinking of direction. He would have to return at least to the edge of the HQ area to get his bearings. But he did not want to come back into the area by Dome Eight. He turned to his left and began to circle around the base of the hill on which the area was located.

A few moments later he came up against a steel fence. He turned and went down along it. A little ways further on he came out of the trees and saw Paumons standing behind the wire mesh of the fence. These must be the prisoners Harmon had been talking about. They stood silently in little clumps. The sun, Bellatrix, was down, but the western sky was still light. In the dusk what little light there was left glimmered here and there on light patches about the prisoners. The patches were bandages that they had put on the wounded by tearing up their own uniforms—dark green on the outside, and light green on the inside—and using them inside out. They stood silently, but he saw them watching him as he passed. In the dusk their figures were outlines, indistinct. They could have been Lehaunan—or humans. He walked on.

"Bunnyrabbit!" said a voice.

The world rocked suddenly. One quick movement. Then it stopped and everything was just the same as it had been a moment before. Cal found he had stopped dead, and his hands were up at his chest, reaching to a harness that was not there. A great chill flowed over him. He turned sharply around.

The dim figures were still there. They did not seem to have moved. A single figure was standing closest to him, back a half a dozen steps, just on the other side of the wire. He went back and looked through the mesh at it. It was a Paumons with a large bandage all over one half of his face. It looked as if he had been badly wounded in the cheek and jaw. He saw the light-colored parts of the Paumons' eyes glitter at him in the gloom.

The Paumons said something. Cal had been taught the language. If what the Paumons had said had been understandable, he would have understood it. But it was not understandable. The other's jaw or tongue must have been damaged to the point of producing incomprehensibility. It was a mangled, bawling sound that made no sense. But it was directed at Cal, and there was a feeling behind it that matched the glitter of the eyes. Cal's ears had metamorphosed it into the recognizable human word.

Cal turned and walked off. After a moment, he stopped, turned and went back, but the prisoner who had spoken to him was no longer at the wire. He looked for a moment at the other motionless shapes, then turned for a final time and went up the slope in the darkness.

The outer office of Dome Eight was still empty, for which he was grateful. Harmon and Alt were still talking behind the partition. He walked up to the door in the parition, and knocked.

There was a pause inside.

"Who's that? Come in!" said Alt. Cal opened the door and stepped a half-step into the inner room. There was a desk at which Harmon was sitting, and Alt was standing half-turned toward the door, in front of the desk. There was a further door and, on the walls, maps and schematics.

"Lieutenant Truant, sir," said Cal. "Contacts Service. I thought I'd better speak to the Colonel. It's about the Paumons prisoners."

Alt turned his head a little bit and looked at Cal more directly.

"Prisoners?"

"Yes, sir."

"What about the prisoners?"

"I happened to pass the compound where they're being held, sir," said Cal. "And some of them spoke to me. You know they gave Contacts trainees the language."

"I know that," said Alt. "What about the prisoners?"

"I thought I'd speak to you, Colonel," said Cal. He looked directly into Alt's face. "The prisoners seem to think something's going to be done with them; they're going to be done away with, or something like that. I thought, as part of elementary Contacts, I might have the Colonel's permission to speak to them on his behalf and assure them they've got nothing to worry about; that they're going to be well treated."

Alt stared at him for a moment.

"You did, did you?" he said.

"Yes, sir."

From behind the desk, Cal could see Harmon also looking at him. The General was tilted a little backwards in his chair, and he had been gazing at Cal all this time with no expression on his face except a sort of steady interest.

"Tell me, Lieutenant," said Alt. "Did you just come in to the outer office, there?"

"Well, yes sir," said Cal. "I did. There was no one out front, so I took a chance and knocked on your door. I didn't realize you were busy with the General."

"That's quite all right," said Harmon. Cal turned his head toward the seated man. "Tell me, aren't you the officer I sent over to see General Scoby, back in Denver?"

"That's right, General."

"I thought so," said Harmon. "I've got quite a good memory for certain things." He sat up straight and businesslike. "Well, Colonel, I think the Lieutenant here should do what he suggests, don't you? We want to make an early start on good Contacts with the Paumons. Wait outside, will you, Lieutenant? The Colonel will have some more specific orders for you as soon as we're done, here."

Cal went out into the outer office and took a chair well away from the partition. He heard the conversation begin again between Harmon and Alt, but the voices were not so loud now and it was not possible to make out the words. After some minutes, the officers and men belonging to the outer office began to come in.

"Did you want to see me, Lieutenant?" asked the Captain at the Liaison Desk—a tall young man with blond hair already veering back at the temples—as he sat down.

"I wanted to locate Contacts HQ," said Cal. "But Colonel Alt asked me to wait on another matter."

"Oh," said the Captain. "Well, Contacts is about three

miles west by the Medics, at Grid four-five-seven-zero.
I imagine Colonel Alt will be calling you shortly."

The lights were all turned up in the outer office,
now, and the four enlisted men and three officers were
all busily at work. Over the noise of their occupation,
Cal heard a door close beyond the partition wall. A
minute or so later, Alt put his head out of the partition
door.

"Truant," he said.

Cal got up and went into the inner office. Alt faced
him inside, his legs a little spread apart, his shoulders
hunched.

"Lieutenant," Alt said. "We're going to get some orders cut for you. You won't have to go back to your
assigned outfit. Those Paumons prisoners you saw are
going to be walked to a Prisoner of War center we're
setting up about forty miles from here at a town called
Manaha. General Harmon suggested, and I agree, that
since POWs generally are handled as a part of Contacts
Service business, you might be the very man to manage
moving them there. The General wants them there by
tomorrow night. We'll give you four armed enlisted
men. You can move out at dawn."

Chapter Eleven

———◆———

Nothing happened in a hurry, of course. Cal's outfit
had to be notified, and the Contacts Service HQ, and

then his orders had to be printed up. It took several hours and as they were just getting into it, the Liaison Desk Captain, who did not seem to share the popular prejudice against Contacts people, suggested Cal see about food and billeting for the night, sending him over to Officers Quarters. Cal got himself allotted a bunk and served some field rations and coffee. The Duty Officer, a young Lieutenant, came in and sat down and had a cup of coffee with him in the empty messroom.

"We'll roll these Progs up in three months," said the Duty Officer. "They've never been hit like this before. It stuns them; and they just give up. I saw them bringing them in all day today."

The Lieutenant was wearing the patch of the Administrative Service.

"Yeah," said Cal. "Can I get some more coffee?"

"Urn's over there. Help yourself," said the Lieutenant.

"Of course, they're aliens. They can't help it. But it may well be practically a bloodless conquest."

As soon as he had his printed orders, Cal went back down to the compound where the prisoners were. He showed the orders to the Section Leader in charge of guarding them.

"I want to talk to their leader," said Cal. The Section unlocked the gate and let him in. There was no illumination inside the fence, but they had set up searchlights outside, and the harsh glare of these cast back a sort of bare stage-lighting over the Paumons standing around in little groups inside. Now that it was illuminated, Cal could see the extent of the compound, which was about five hundred feet on the square. The only structures inside it were a sanitation dome, and a small office dome.

"I want to talk to your ranking officer," said Cal in Paumons, to the figures nearest to him. Without waiting for an answer, he went on into the office dome, which had a table and a few chairs, and sat down behind the table.

After a few minutes the door opened and two unwounded Paumons came in and stood before the desk. At first glance they looked alike as all the others did. But Cal, searching hard for differences, saw that the one facing him on the right was a little taller and stood straighter. The one on the left, without any particular identifiable sign of it, gave an impression of greater age. They both wore the piping on their trousers and jacket battle dress that identified them as officers.

"Sit down," said Cal in Paumons, indicating two chairs he had arranged on the other side of the desk.

"No," said the one on the right. "I am General Commander Wantaki. This is my aide, Leader Ola Tain."

"All right," said Cal. "I'm the officer who is going to be responsible for moving everybody in this compound to more permanent quarters tomorrow. We will move out at dawn."

"Everyone?" said Wantaki. "A good quarter of the men here are walking wounded, and there are close to seven sixes of men who cannot walk."

"That's why I am talking to you tonight," said Cal. "It is a very long day's march to where we are going, even for your well people. But I have my orders and I must carry them out. I will do what I can, but you must all travel. So I tell you now."

"What good does that do?" said Wantaki harshly.

"Listen," cautioned his companion, Ola Tain, who had not spoken up until now.

"I suggest you make preparations," said Cal. "Rig litters and assign those who are well to help the walking wounded. I have already arranged to have litter poles and fabric for the litters and for bandages to be given you."

"You show an unusual amount of courage to come in

here without at least a sidearm," said Wantaki. "Some of my people, and I do not exclude myself, might not be able to resist the temptation."

"I belong to a branch of the human army known as the Contacts Service," said Cal. "The Contacts Service never bears arms or joins in the fighting."

"They would be well advised to change their ways in the seasons to come," said Wantaki. "If you supply us with poles and fabric, we will use them. Is that all?"

"That is all," said Cal. They went out. He himself went out and returned to the gate. The Section Leader of the Guard let him out.

"I've made arrangements with Quartermaster to have some litter materials and stuff delivered to the prisoners," Cal told him. "Let it through to them when it comes."

He went back to Officers Quarters and turned in to his assigned bunk. He went off to sleep immediately, but several hours later he was awakened by the Duty Officer.

"What's up?" said Cal thickly. Ugly dark half-remembered shapes were still thronging the back of his brain.

"You were yelling," said the Duty Officer. "Some kind of a nightmare or something, about rabbits."

In the pale light of predawn, near the fence, Cal could see the four armed men he had been given to control the five-hundred-odd prisoners on the march. He imagined Alt had personally selected them. Two were youngsters. One had his hair cropped to a stubble and a thin, wide, sharp-looking mouth in a thin face. The other was small and large-eyed. One was on the same type and age as Mahauni, the mulebrain who had taken over command of the outfit under the torps. These were all buck soldiers. There was a non-com, too, a Squad-man. He was lanky, black-haired, and tall. He did not call the men to attention as Cal came up, but stayed lounging against the fence above the other three seated on the grass. They were all wearing full harness and weapons.

"You the prisoner guard?" said Cal as he came up.

"That's us," drawled the non-com, not moving, glancing at Cal's Contacts Service patch.

"What's your name?" Cal asked him.

"My friends call me Buck," said the Squadman. Cal waited. "Allen," said the Squadman.

"All right, Allen," said Cal, in the same tone of voice. "You report back to your outfit and tell them to send me somebody else. Tell them you impressed me as being sloppy, unreliable and insubordinate, and that I said I couldn't use you."

Allen straightened up with a jerk.

"Hey, wait a minute—" he began. But Cal was turning to the other three.

"On your feet," he said. They scrambled up. Behind him, Cal heard the Squadman talking.

". . . senior man of the Combat Services gives the orders in the field. You don't tell me—"

Cal looked around. "I thought I gave you an order," he said.

"Listen, Lieutenant, I—"

"Get in there," said Cal, turning back to the three others. "Start counting the prisoners, and see that all the wounded who can't walk have litters." They went off.

Cal watched them go down the fence, in through the gate and out of earshot. The Squadman was still talking. He stopped when he saw Cal's face.

"Listen," said Cal, holding his voice down. He could feel his arms beginning to shake from the tensed muscles in them. "Listen, soldier. Get one thing clear in that head of yours. You're here to do what I tell you, and exactly what I tell you in getting these prisoners to Manaha. You can just forget anything else. Never mind

rule books or the kind of Contacts Officers you maybe
ran into in the past. Just remember that on the official papers it's just you and me, all alone on this trip.
And if you think your two stripes can play games with
these"—Cal jabbed a rod-stiff finger at his Lieutenant's
tabs—"just you try it. And I'll hang your hind end, boy.
Remember that. No matter what happens to me, when
the dust settles you're going to find yourself in front of
a long table with five officers of the rank of major or
above behind it."

Cal quit talking. He was shaking all over now. He
knew Allen could see it, but he didn't give a damn.

"Well?" he said. Allen was not moving. He stood
stiff and stared straight ahead. His face was pale. "All
right," said Cal, almost in a whisper. "I'm going to take
you along and you're going to see that you and those
other three do the job they're supposed to do. Now, get
in there and get them organized."

Allen turned and went. Cal watched him go, and
gradually the case of shakes he had picked up began
to leak out of him.

They actually got the Paumons prisoners moving by
half an hour after sunrise, which was even better than
Cal had hoped. He had figured it would take a full
hour to get the march actually on the road. What
helped was the authority of Wantaki and Ola Tain. They
had taken over internal command of the march; and
Cal wisely let them be.

He and his four soldiers wore jump belts; and he
had a man pogo-sticking along on each side of the
column, one at the rear and Allen up front. He jumped
back and forth from tail to rear of the marching
column, himself.

It was a good-weather day; there was that much in
its favor. They were in the southern latitudes of the
northern hemisphere and high up. The air was dry. To

begin with, the column made nearly three miles an hour, but that could not last, Cal thought. He moved back and forth along one side of the column, then in the opposite direction along the other. The Paumons prisoners marched steadily, in a rough column of fours, two whole individuals on each side of a wounded, two frequently changed on each litter. Their eyebrowless, dish-shaped faces seemed to show no expression. They talked little among themselves. He found himself getting curious about them.

There was an atmosphere of numbness about them, a leaden quality. They marched like people in a dream, or about some dreary, routine task. Only up at the head of the column were exceptions to this to be found. There, Wantaki strode with heavy, jarring footfalls, staring straight ahead like a thwarted wrestler. Beside him, Ola Tain paced soberly, but apparently calmly.

Now that Cal had time to study the two leaders, he found himself puzzled by Ola Tain. Wantaki he could understand to a certain extent. The Paumons Commander had the ring of the military about him. But Ola Tain did not seem to belong at all. He was almost like a priest.

They had been stopping at Cal's order ten minutes out of every hour. They also stopped at noon. Nobody had known anything about rations for the prisoners, or even what the Paumons ate, when Cal had asked about it back at HQ before leaving. So the column was without food. They did not complain about it, but sat quietly in the brilliant, high-altitude sunlight from small, bright Bellatrix, like a white coin in the sky. Glanced at for just a fraction of a second, it left a black after-image burning against the closed eyelid, floating about with the hidden movements of the eyeballs.

When the order came to move on, they took up their march again. But they were definitely slowing. It was the wounded who were holding the rest back. They went through several small towns, but the white, low buildings on either side of the narrow, winding streets were locked up tight and no Paumons civilians showed themselves. By mid-afternoon, Cal was forced to call another halt and the prisoners, particularly the litter-bearers, went down where they stood as if they had been so much grain cut by a scythe.

Cal sat on a little rise of ground at the side of the road and let them lie. After about twenty minutes, Allen came up to him.

"How long we going to leave them here, Lieutenant?" the Squadman asked. Cal looked up at the man without answering, and Allen wet his lips and went away.

It occurred to Cal that he had no idea how much endurance the Paumons might have. It might be less, or more, than humans in the same position. He got up and went up to the head of the column. Wantaki was there, sitting on a roadside boulder, looking back over the column of men. One muddy, rust-colored hand was on his knee, curled up into a fist. His face was as hard and washed clean as a stone seen under running water in a mountain stream fed by glaciers. He sat alone. Ola Tain was a little ways off, also alone, lying on a hill-side. Cal turned and went toward Tain.

They had come to a wide open area of the plateau now, with only an occsional clump of the cottonwood trees. In between the heaved up rock, in the stony soil, the green moss was everywhere. There was a faint, sweet odor to it, like lavender.

The moss deadened the sound of Cal's footsteps, and Ola Tain evidently did not hear him approaching. The Paumons aide was lying on one elbow, the forefinger of the hand belonging to that elbow tracing out the small, feathery stems of the moss-plant directly underneath it. His face was absorbed. Cal's steps slowed as he watched the other. For the first time, now, he saw that there were tiny yellow blossoms hidden among the cone-shaped leaves of each miniature stem, and that Ola Tain's finger was counting these.

Cal felt a constriction in his guts and his throat tightened. There came to him suddenly a strong and desperate longing to know what sort of feelings moved inside the breathing, living being just a few feet from him; a sort of terrible loneliness. He opened his mouth to speak, but all that happened was that he made a sound in his throat. Ola Tain looked up.

"I need some information," said Cal, in Paumons. "I did not think now would be a good time to ask the General Commander."

Ola Tain's glance slid past Cal to Wantaki, and back to Cal again.

"No," he said.

"I want to know," said Cal, "how your people are standing up to the march. We have still over half the distance to go."

"You see," said Ola Tain, nodding toward the column. "Can you tell us what our destination is?"

"Manaha. I have no means to take care of stragglers."

"I had noticed that." Ola Tain looked at him for a moment. "You are doing the best you can for us within your orders?"

"Yes."

"I had thought so, myself. I will help as I can."

"If we take until tomorrow dawn, will all make it?"

"We will pray so."

Cal lingered, looking down at him.

"You pray?" he said.

"Sometimes," said Ola Tain. "I am praying today."

"What to?"

"Does it matter?" said Ola Tain.

"I guess not." Cal looked back over the column, then down at Ola Tain again. "You're a strange sort of soldier."

"I am not really a soldier. I teach—" the term he gave did not translate well. Something between philosophy and anthropology, in the Paumons sense.

"*He* is a soldier," Cal nodded toward Wantaki. "He hates us, doesn't he?"

"Yes," said Ola Tain.

"Do you hate us?"

"I try not to. Hate gets in the way of clear thinking. But . . ." Ola Tain hesitated. "Yes, I hate you, too." He looked back down at the flowers of the moss.

"Well," said Cal, after a second, "we're only ensuring the safety of our bases and our people, you know."

"Please." Ola Tain did not look up. "Do not make it harder for me to try not to hate you."

Cal went back to the column, and to Squadman Allen.

"Get 'em moving," he said.

With the declining of the sun, the air cooled quickly. At first that seemed to have a good effect on the prisoners and revived the column. But as Bellatrix sought the horizon, what had been merely a pleasant coolness now began to approach a chilliness. With the long night ahead of him, Cal faced the fact that the only way to keep the most of his prisoners moving was to get some food and drink into them.

He took Ola Tain and went ahead up to the next town. Together and alone, they came on the small place by surprise. There were lights in the windows and female Paumons and children moving about the streets. They stared for a moment at the sight of Cal, then scattered to their buildings. Ola Tain left him and went on into the heart of the town, alone.

He was some little time getting back. When he returned, he was followed by a female driving a civilian balloon-tired transport carrying food and drink of the Paumons variety.

"Well, you got it," said Cal to Ola Tain, as they

headed back toward the column with the truck going ahead.

"With your people attacking, they did not want to spare it," said Ola Tain, looking ahead to the truck. "It is not easy." After a moment, he said, "I had to threaten them with you."

They got back to the column, which had built fires. After the prisoners had eaten, they appeared stronger. But at the next halt, Allen came up to Cal.

"There's five of them dead," he said. "They've been carrying them all this time in the litters so we'd think they were wounded."

"If they can keep up, let them," said Cal.

But during the long night, the column began to straggle. Cal ordered the dead left behind, and in the process found that there were now twelve corpses in the column. They left them behind and went on, the exhausted, four to a litter now, carrying the near-dead, the staggering wounded helping each other. Cal increased his halts to one every half-hour.

Dawn found them straggling through another small town. Word of their movement had gone ahead of them over the civilian Paumons communications system, which was still operating. With Manaha, their destination, only a little over two miles off, the civilians had grown bolder and more in sympathy with the prisoners. They said nothing, but they peered from windows and rooftops, and dodged up side streets out of the way, as the column reeled forward.

As they emerged from the last village before Manaha, they found the road ahead lined with the old, the female and the young. They moved back from the road as Allen, leading the column, came toward them, but they waved in again toward the plodding prisoners as he passed. Looking ahead now, along the semi-open country ahead, Cal could see the distant glint of sun on windows that would be Manaha. He looked back at the reeling column; at the civilian Paumons, leaning in toward it as if over some invisible barrier rope. Wantaki and Ola Tain still moved ahead of the rest.

There was a slight bend in the road, and, as Allen reached it, the crowd of Paumons children there shrank back. But as he passed on, they bulged forward. There was a sudden flurry in their ranks, and a small, male youngster darted toward Ola Tain, who was closest.

The thin young soldier with the wide mouth snapped up his machine pistol.

"Hold it!" shouted Cal, as the youngster darted back again into the safety of the crowd, leaving Ola Tain holding a green and leafy branch from one of the cottonwood-type trees. For a long moment Ola Tain looked at it in his hands; and then, holding it upright before him, took up the march again.

A moment later, another child, a little older this time, darted out with a branch for Wantaki.

Soon, branches were being delivered to prisoners, all along the column. Allen came back to Cal.

"Sir?" he said, looking at Cal.

"Leave them alone," said Cal harshly.

Allen went back to the head of the column. Soon all the prisoners had branches. Each carried his own upright before him, their shoulders straightened, and stepping out. As they came into Manaha at last, they looked like a forest on the move. And they were marching like soldiers.

Chapter Twelve

Cal rejoined his outfit after that, and for the next six months he worked with Battalion as Interpreter, questioning prisoners. The Expedition made large advances, conquering most of the planet. It went as Harmon had predicted. The Paumons had to come to the Expedition on the plateau, and the Expedition made large-scale drops of fighting forces elsewhere around the world.

But it was not a bloodless conquest. It took the Paumons some time to learn not to fight head-on battles against the vastly superior equipment of the Expedition, that whenever they did they suffered heartbreaking losses. The Expedition also suffered losses. At the end of six months they had received three sets of replacements for the Combat Services; their casualties were over seventy-five thousand. Estimates of the Paumons casualties put those at over two million dead and wounded. Cal was promoted twice, to first Leiutenant and then to Captain, and was brought back to take charge of the big new Prisoner-of-War center next to Expedition Headquarters and Expedition Main Hospital at Manaha. This gave him a chance to be with Annie, who was stationed at Main Hospital. He heard occasionally of Walk, who was making a name for himself as commander of a newly formed guerrilla-hunting group. Promotions had been faster in the Combat Services, and Walk had made major.

One day Annie called Cal from over at Hospital Receiving to say they had just brought Walk in with multiple wounds of the arm and leg from a Paumons mortar. Cal juggled his schedule for the day and went over to the hospital. He found Walk had already been put into a room by himself. In the anteroom outside were Annie, who was charting up the readings of the preliminary checkover the Medical Officer had given Walk, and a Public Relations Officer from Administrative, who was there to write him up for a news release back on Earth.

"Can I go in and see him?" Cal asked Annie.

"In a minute," she said, coding up results of the checkover, with her fingers hopping over the machine keys. "I'll take you in. I asked to be his nurse."

"Are you a buddy of his?" asked the PR Officer, a neat First Lieutenant with a mustache. "The officers and men of his outfit idolize him, I hear. And to the Paumons he's almost a legend they tell to frighten their children into being good. Maybe we can get some pictures of the two of you together. His story is one long string of heroic exploits after another. They say even the aliens respect him."

"You can come in now," said Annie to Cal. They went in together. Walk was lying in a hospital bed, under a light top sheet only. He was so tanned and thin he looked like a sun-blackened corpse against the white sheets. His eyes focused crazily on Cal as he came up to the side of the bed.

"Cal . . ." he muttered. "What're you doing here? Get out. . . . Get back to base. . . ."

"He's out of his head," said Annie. She folded Walk's arm up and put a hypodermic syringe gun against the side of it. After a moment his eyes began to clear. He recognized Cal sensibly, and his lips twisted in a hard line.

"Captain Truant," he said.

"How're you feeling?" asked Cal.

"Like a million," said Walk. "Just like a million." He made an effort to pull himself up on his pillow. "Nurse—" He recognized Annie. "Annie, they got any liquor around here for the casualties?"

"I'm sorry," said Annie, "but they've got to do some operating on you."

". . . them," said Walk. His tongue was beginning to thicken. Annie had evidently given him some fast-acting sedation. ". . . you, too. All of you . . . The universe. That's all it's good for. . . ."

His eyes closed and he passed out. Annie put a gentle hand on Cal's arm.

"That's all right," said Cal. "It doesn't matter. I was figuring he'd be like this."

He went back to his office at the POW compound. There was a message that General Scoby wanted to see him, but Ola Tain had been waiting in his outer office for half an hour. In the large Manaha POW Center that now held over eighty thousand Paumons, Ola Tain was Cal's most valuable connection. It was as Scoby had implied in his talk with Cal after Cal had graduated from Contacts School, back in Denver. There were no rules for building a basis for co-existence with those you had conquered. You could only feel your way.

Cal felt it mainly through Ola Tain. Wantaki had escaped early. He and five of his officers had broken out and got clean away the second week of their internment at Manaha. Cal was convinced that Ola Tain could have gone at that time, also, if he had wanted to. But he had chosen to stay and speak for the other prisoners. The other prisoners seemed to respect him, but not absorb him. It was as if he was alien to them, too. Cal had asked once if he was never lonely.

"No," said Ola Tain. "One can only be lonely within walls. And I have never built any."

Now Cal stopped in the outer office to explain that he would have to get over and see Scoby.

"There's no hurry about my business," said Ola Tain. "I have only promised to ask again that the recreation area be enlarged."

"I'll ask General Scoby about it," said Cal.

He went on over to Contacts Service HQ. Scoby, busy at his desk as Cal came in, looked as if he, his office, and Limpari the cheetah had been transported all in a package from Denver, without even disturbing the papers piled on the desk. Cal repeated Ola Tain's request.

"No," replied Scoby. He leaned back in his chair and stared at Cal, seated opposite him. "They don't really want more space. They just want to find out if the rumor's true."

"What rumor?"

"That if peace is signed next month, they'll all be released."

"I hadn't heard that."

"It's circulating," said Scoby. "What do you think we ought to do about it?"

"Do?" said Cal.

"That's what I said."

"Nothing. The whole thing's crazy. In the first place we're a lot more than a month from signing peace, anyway. Wantaki's still back in those mountains of Zone Eleven with better than thirty thousand men."

"Thirty thousand isn't much," said Scoby with one of his sudden spasms of mildness. "They can be ignored. The main civilian Paumons representatives are ready to ignore him and sign."

"You mean they'd leave him in the position of an outlaw—the Commander that fought harder for them than anyone else? Him and thirty thousand men, to say nothing of all the other guerrilla groups around the world?"

"They're a lot like us," said Scoby. "Or hadn't you noticed?"

"I noticed," said Cal bitterly.

Scoby gazed at him for a moment.

"Trouble with you, Cal," he said, "is you're still expecting miracles from people—and I mean people of all sorts, Lehaunan, Griella, Paumons, as well as human. That's the trouble with most of us. We quit expecting the worst from people, so right away we've got to swing over and start expecting nothing but the best."

"If the General will forgive me," said Cal. "I'll try to do better next time."

"And don't get sarcastic. You've learned a lot this last year but I still know a few things more than you do. One of them is how particularly important this particular race is to us. Or can you tell me that too?"

Cal thought a moment.

"No," he said, finally, "I guess not."

"They're important just because they are so damn much like us," said Scoby. "Long as the races we were knocking over were covered with fur, or had prehensile noses, we could go on calling them Pelties or Anteaters. We could shut our eyes to the fact that they had about as much brains, or probably about as much soul as we had. But an alien we got to call 'Prog', now—that's getting a little like 'God' or 'Nigger.' You're sort of straining to point up the difference. And yet it stood to reason if we were going to bump into other thinking races out among the stars, sooner or later one of them was bound to be pretty human."

He stopped. He looked at Cal for a reaction.

"I guess you're right," said Cal.

"Of course," said Scoby, "I'm using the word *human* in only its finest sense."

"I guessed you were," said Cal. "So being like us is what makes the Paumons so important?"

"That's right," said Scoby. "What would you do if you were a Paumons and this was Earth, and you had eighty thousand 'Humies' out behind that wire when peace was signed? Would you want to turn them loose?"

Cal straightened up in his chair.

"Hell, no!" he said. "I see what you mean."

"Not unless you wanted to start the conquest all over again, that right?" said Scoby. "How far would you say these people are from being re-educated into living side by side with us?"

"Twenty years," said Cal. "Do something with the next generation maybe."

"Don't kid yourself. Five generations'll have a hard time wiping out the fact we started things out by coming in and trompling them."

"Can you talk General Harmon out of releasing them?"

"No."

"Then we're helpless," said Cal. "We're just giving them back an army. This and the other POW camps—they'll have three-quarters of a million men under arms again in half a year. And we can't do a thing."

"Not quite," said Scoby. "Once peace is signed, Contacts Service Head can interdict any step taken by Combat Services Commander, if Contacts Head thinks it'll lead to a breach of the peace."

"Ouch," said Cal. "But you wouldn't want to do that to Harmon."

"No. But then I won't have to," said Scoby. "You will."

Cal sat up straighter suddenly. He stared at Scoby, but Scoby was not smiling.

"Me?" Cal said.

"I told you I'd been grooming you," said Scoby. "I've got men here who've been with me sixteen years. But you've got the Combat experience, and you've got the guts. You've got something else, too."

"But me—" said Cal, and stopped.

"Every Expedition the mulebrains in the field talk about how they should all hang together and go back as a unit to straighten out the ex-mulies in Government. The man on the spot always thinks he know best. Rubs Government the wrong way. It's happening now—politics, boy. Now's the time for me to get things from Government. I've got to go back to Earth and fight for our team."

"I'm not sure I can do that," said Cal slowly.

"I'm sure for you," said Scoby. "I'm having orders cut now, giving you a double jump to Lieutenant Colonel. You'll have as much authority here as I would—just not the reputation to back it up. That you've got to make yourself." Scoby grinned. "Be happy, boy. You're going up in the world."

Chapter Thirteen

———◆———

Cal saw Scoby off from the Headquarters field just outside Manaha. The field had been leveled and poured only six months before. But the green moss could grow anywhere, and where it was not burnt away daily by the ascending ships, it had flung long arms across the concrete. It was destroyed by a puff of heat, the touch of a human foot. But it grew again overnight. Standing

with Scoby, waiting for boarding orders to be announced
on the slim, small courier ship that would take the older
man home, Cal could see, less than forty yards away,
the great tower of the Expedition's flagship black against
the morning sky. It had not moved since landing on this
spot eleven days, local time, after the first drops in
which Cal had come down with Wajeck and the others.
It carried the sheathed sword of nuclear explosives
under its armor, that could potentially devastate the
world it stood on for half a thousand miles in every
direction from where it stood. It could wound a planet;
and from four hundred and twenty-six feet above Cal
and Scoby, in the observation room, the single caretaker
soldier aboard it could be looking down on them all.
From the main screen he could be seeing the lesser ships
below him, and the field, and Manaha, with all the
main strength of the Expedition laid out like a toy
scale model below. And even on this lord of space and
war, the moss at its base was already beginning to lay
its tender, green relentless fingers.

The hooter sounded, announcing boarding orders.

"Hold hard, Cal," said Scoby, one fist clutching the
handle of Limpari's harness. He put his hand out blindly, and Cal took it. In the last moment one of his blackouts had taken him and he could not see. They shook.
"Now, girl," he muttered to Limpari. And smoothly
and powerfully, she led him away from Cal and onto
the ship.

Cal went back to Contacts HQ and a work day that
in the several months following stretched to better than
ten hours as a routine matter. He had little time even
to see Annie. He had come to depend on her heavily,
but when she suggested that they might get married—he
had never mentioned it—the violence of his reaction
startled even him.

"No!" he had shouted at her. "Not now! Can't you see that? Not now!"

He had turned and flung himself three angry strides away from her, from the hospital desk where she was sitting on duty, at the moment she had mentioned it. Down the hall, an ambulatory patient had turned, surprised, to stare. Ashamed suddenly, he came back to the desk, but muttering under his breath still, "Not now. Now's not the time, Annie. Can't you see that?"

She did not press him.

The peace was signed. Wantaki was now an outlaw in Zone Eleven, with now nearly twenty thousand Paumons. Walk, recovered, was also back in Zone Eleven, harrying the Paumons leader from a series of strong posts encircling the base of the mountains. Harmon signed the order releasing all Paumons prisoners of war, and Cal stood at his office window and watched as the waves of prisoners celebrating their release literally tore the gates from their hinges and ripped half the compound to shreds along with it. For a day and a night, riot threatened in and around Manaha. Three mechanized battalions were ordered in to patrol the area. Subdued, the Paumons ex-prisoners melted away to their own home area. Five days later, Cal looked out at the torn and empty shells of the buildings in the compound as rain began to fall.

The initial drops of the Expedition had been timed to come at the earliest possible date after the winter season on this plateau. Now a new winter season—a time of rain—was upon the high, arid country about. Day in and day out, the gray curtains of the rain obscured the landscape as Cal went back and forth between Contacts HQ, Expeditions HQ, the Medical Center, and his own quarters.

For two months the rainy season continued. Meanwhile, elsewhere about the planet, the yeast of the returned Paumons fighting men was beginning to ferment.

The Paumons civilian authorities made apparently honest attempts to comply with the plan for reorganization and re-education of their people. But the whole planet now was beginning to quake and gasp from unexpected fumaroles, like cooking oatmeal before it comes to an active boil. The Paumons people were torn, divided and violent. On the one hand there were outlaw resistance groups even in the large cities, haunted by human soldiery and their own police as well. On the other hand, in Zone Eleven, Walk commanded one whole fighting unit made up of Paumons enlistees and ex-soldiers. Ugly stories began to emerge from Zone Eleven, and from the activities of resistance groups elsewhere. Prisoners were not taken so often; and those who were taken by both sides were liable to turn up later as corpses in not-so-pretty condition.

Cal, trapped in a snarl of paperwork and tripped up on every hand by inefficiency or petty resentment on the part of Contacts Officers over whose head Scoby had promoted him by putting him in Paumons authority, saw a crisis approaching. He messaged Scoby back on Earth, saying that the greater authority of the older man was badly needed with the Expedition. Scoby sent back word that he could not possibly come before six weeks. Talk to Harmon, he advised. Cal made an attempt to do so, but his appointments with the Commander of the Expedition had a way of being canceled at the last moment. Harmon messaged that he would have his office set up time for a talk with Cal at the first opportunity. Time slipped by.

The six weeks came and went. Harmon remained incommunicative. Scoby had not come, or sent word he was coming. Cal, working alone in his office early one evening—he understood better now why Scoby's desk had always been loaded with papers—at endless reports and explanations of reports, heard the single snap of a fire rifle close under his window. And then two more snaps.

There was a commotion in his outer office. His door burst open, and a Paumons whom he suddenly recognized as Ola Tain half-fell inside. There was a babble of voices beyond in the outer office as Cal jumped up and helped the other into a chair. Ola Tain was burnt clear through the body twice. He could not live. The office door banged open again, and Cal, looking up, saw a hard-faced and shoulder-scorched man in the entrance whom he did not recognize—and then with a sudden shock did recognize. He had looked a little like Walk, but he was Washun, the Contacts Cadet who had shared Cal's second tour of Basic at Fort Cota. The Contacts shoulder patch on his jacket now was stained and ancient.

"It's Walker Blye, in Zone Eleven," said Washun. "He's planning a massacre."

Chapter Fourteen

The two-man atmosphere ship fled westward at forty thousand feet of altitude. It caught up with the retreating sunset, passed it and came down half a world away in late afternoon at Garrison Number Three of Zone Eleven—Walk's Headquarters.

The garrison was drained empty of men. The senior man was a non-com, a Wing Section. It was Tack. He

and Cal looked at each other like close relatives that
have been raised at far distances from each other, and
to different customs, as Cal questioned him.

"He left six hours since," said Tack. "He took twen-
ty-eight hundred men and all equipment back in the
hills. To that place they call the Valley of the Three
Towns—how did you know?"

"A Paumons named Ola Tain," said Cal. "Wantaki
knows about Walk's plan. Was he crazy? He could be
court-martialed for this."

"He *is* crazy," said Tack, lowering his voice, and
glancing at Washun, who had made the trip with Cal,
and now stood at the long end of the Headquarters
Office, out of earshot. "He doesn't care—about anything. And he's always drunk, now. But you say Wantaki's laying for him?"

"Yes," said Cal. His body felt heavy and tired and
old. "Tain came to your own Contacts man in this
area"—he gestured at Washun—"to try and stop the
whole thing. But your tame Paumons caught him and
shot him up. Washun rescued him and got him to me.
But he couldn't even talk by that time." Cal felt bitter
inside. "He was shot again outside my office by some
fool."

"Can you get to Walk in time?"

"Give me a combat-ground car. I'll try."

The sunset caught up with Cal once more as he
shoved the little ground car, alone, along an unpaved
roadway back into the jagged, tree-covered young mountains of Zone Eleven. In the darkness, the trees looked
even more like Earthly trees, the dirt road like some
back-country trail of home. The combat car, fleeing a
few inches above the pounded dirt of the road on the
soft, shushing noise of its countless tiny jets, seemed to
be pouring itself into the pit of the quickly falling darkness. And there came on Cal suddenly one of those

seconds of strange emotion he had been used to calling
"inside-out" moments when he was a boy—while his
mother was still alive. For the first time he recognized
that he had never had them after her death. But now
one was with him once again and he saw himself with a
strange, still, twilight clarity, as if from a little distance, a different viewpoint just outside his body. And
what he saw had a sadly comical lack of sense and
yet a sharp understanding.

What, he wondered suddenly, was he doing here in
this heavy, adult body? In a complicated vehicle, on
this strange world, upon this alien soil? To what dan-
gerous explosion of things were the steel bars of events
channeling him? He was bound to save some lives, to
avert some kind of disaster. But was that really the purpose, was that really the meaning? For a moment he
found himself storm-tossed on a sea of endless mystery.
And then the road curved suddenly and his own automatic hands, jerking the combat car into the turn,
snapped things sharply into pitilessly clear and unam-
biguous focus in his mind.

It was not any faceless duty that he was facing here,
but the sharp spectre of his own guilt. It was not the
Paumons villages, but Walk he was rushing to save, so
that he might still save himself.

For it was Walk, his dark twin; Walk, his other self,
for whom he was responsible and had always been responsible. Annie had seen it, when she had burst out
in the hospital back on Earth after the Lehaunan expedition, that Walk was the weak one. Weak he was
not, in the ordinary sense. But when they had gravitated
together instinctively as boys—two motherless half-or-
phans—Walk had been the one with greater need and
less initiative of imagination. Cal had taken the Services' side in revenge against his father for his mother's death. But Walk, following Cal's greater imagination
into the glory-land of a military life which Cal had

fashioned as a club against Cal's father, had had no buried knowledge of its unreality outside Cal's mind. Walk had believed. He had followed the sound of the trumpet, expecting to find the home and the kin he lacked behind it. And Cal, who had known his lie for what it was from the beginning, deep inside, had escaped his own mirage—but left Walk behind with it, stumbling in the desert.

Walk had pursued the mirage of love, and, not finding it, had grown more savage and murderous. He would *force* the mirage to be real. He would *force* his cause to be just, his fighting noble, his life, when it came to an end, to be a worthy price paid on a purchase of value. And all the time he was doing this, the undeniable realization grew stronger and stronger in him that his god was an empty shell, his purposes false, and he faced no final dedication, but the closed-in grave of a brain-mad wolf.

But the sin in this, it came home to Cal now, was on Cal's head. For whatever small credit, he might try to count work he had done with the Paumons prisoners of war. For whatever Paumons soldiers he had saved on that march to Manaha, or eased in better conditions of prison camps, or protected during questioning by Combat officers; for whatever he might count to his benefit from this—he must also count his share in the Paumons whom Walk had harried to an exhausted end, to those prisoners who had died from indifference or cruelty while in his hands, to those he had slain outright, or killed for no necessary reason. If Walk massacred tonight, Cal massacred also.

Cal's hands were wet with sweat on the wheel. Night had completely fallen. As recklessly as Walk himself might have done, Cal flung the combat car into the turns and twists of the unknown and narrow road, toward its destination.

Through the darkness, with only the narrow beam of

his headlights, he fled. Finally, he nosed upward over a little rise and saw abruptly down into a valley where lights glowed and clustered about three main areas. He swooped down upon them. But as he entered the first of these, he found the lights came from the broken windows of damaged homes. There was rubble in the streets, but no movement of living beings. But when he stopped in the little open space at the center of the town area where he was, dark bodies moved in around his car.

He got out. They were all Paumons laden with weapons.

"Come," said one of them. Cal followed him. They walked across the open space, and Cal's guide stood aside at a door to a low building. Cal pushed open the door and stepped inside. He found himself in a low-roofed room with a dirt floor. There was a wooden table, two cots, some plain chairs, and several heavy, square wooden timbers holding up the roof. Wantaki stood beside the table, and between two of the pillars, slumped with the cords about his wrists only holding him upright, his shirt torn off, was Walk.

"Ola Tain?" said Wantaki. Cal, who had started to go to Walk, stopped. He had thought Walk unconscious when he first stepped in, but he saw now that although Walk's head slumped between his bare shoulders, his eyes were open and watching. His body showed a bad wound low on the left side.

"Dead," said Cal. "He died reaching me."

"Yes," said Wantaki. He did not say anything more for a moment. "I would have saved him, but . . . that is the way it goes for people like him."

Cal came up to the table. Wantaki looked squarely at him.

"I have no good word to say for you," said Wantaki. "People like you are—" the Paumons expression he used was untranslatable. "With him"—he used the verb form that made it clear he was referring to Walk, the only other person in the room—"it is different. He is as good as a man any day. If you had been all like that, you might even have eaten us up the way you have tried to. But you were not. I would not even have him tied up like that, but many of my soldiers hate him, and something had to be done."

He waited. Cal waited also, saying nothing.

"I am a military man," said Wantaki. "This is the beginning. For a while your weapons gave you an advantage; but we have stolen some of them and made more. Today was the beginning. We are going to rise all over the world. We will wipe out your Expedition. And then we will go hunting you in your own home planet."

"No," said Cal. "Any uprising will fail. The Expedition has weapons it has not used."

"I do not believe you," said Wantaki. He stared at Cal for a long moment. "Besides it does not matter. Weapons can eventually be duplicated. If we fail this time, we will not fail next. The Paumons spirit will never endure to be a tame beast. And right is on our side."

"That can only end in a stalemate," said Cal.

"How can it end in a stalemate when we are superior to you?" said Wantaki. "Given equal weapons, our spirit will conquer—I do not know why I talk to you."

"I do," said Cal. "You're thinking of all the Paumons that must die before you win your victory." He stepped to the edge of the table. "If the humans would negotiate with you, face to face, as equals, and not as conquerors talking to conquered, would you hold off your rising?"

Wantaki said nothing.

"If you could walk into Expedition Headquarters with sufficient force to feel safe, and there talk, would you?"

"You cannot do this," said Wantaki.

"I can. Give me three days." Cal looked over at Walk. "And him."

"He is dying."

"Still."

Wantaki stepped away from the table and then stepped back again.

"I have a responsibility to save lives, as you say," he said. "I don't believe you . . . but it's a bargain." He went to the door. "When you are ready to go, you may go."

He went out. Cal turned quickly to Walk and untied the rope on one side. Walk came heavily down into his arms. Holding him, Cal got the other rope untied and laid Walk on one of the cots. Walk's eyelids fluttered and he looked up into Cal's face.

Walk's lips moved. He did not seem to be saying anything. Then Cal realized he was whispering. Cal bent his ear down close to the lips.

"Cal," Walk was whispering. ". . . lucky . . . lucky, go out . . . in . . . time."

"You're going to be all right," said Cal. Then he realized from the shadow of a look on Walk's face that he had misunderstood. It was not the present moment Walk was talking about.

". . . lies," whispered Walk. ". . . trumpets . . . drums. Liars . . ."

"Lie quiet," said Cal. "Rest a bit. Then I'm taking you east to the Hospital."

Walk sighed and closed his eyes and lay still. Cal sat quietly beside him for perhaps half an hour. Then he realized Walk had opened his eyes and was looking at him again.

"What?" said Cal. He bent down to hear. Walk's faint breath tickled his ear.

"Annie . . ." whispered Walk, ". . . hates me?"

"No," said Cal. "Hell, no! Annie likes you. We both like you a lot. So does Tack. So does everybody."

"Good," Walk whispered. ". . . know . . . somebody. You . . . never . . . ?"

"Hell, no!"

"Promised me . . . good . . . feeling. Noble . . . Liars. Feel lousy . . . dying. Nothing but . . . damnservice. . . ."

"Hey, boy," said Cal. His throat hurt. He reached out and took hold of Walk's hand. "You got nothing but family. Annie, and me and everybody. What're you talking about?"

"Lousy . . . Knew . . . liars, long . . . time ago. Didn't get out . . . time." He closed his eyes once more and lay still.

Cal continued to sit. About an hour later, Walk spoke once more.

"Don't . . . mind . . . being killed," Cal was barely able to make out with his ear right at the pale lips. "Just . . . don't want . . . to die. . . ."

A little while later, when Cal lifted an eyelid, the eye beneath stared straight and unmoving and fixed.

Chapter Fifteen

Cal brought the body of Walk into Hospital Receiving, back at the Hospital at Expedition Headquarters.

"But the man's dead, Colonel!" said the First Lieutenant in Receiving. "What do you want us to do with him?"

"Give him a Services funeral," said Cal. He went in search of Annie.

"I'm going to see Harmon," he said. "I want you to get off duty here, now, and do something for me. Can you do that?"

"Yes," she said. "What is it, Cal?"

"Get a ground car and follow me over. Wait until I go in to Headquarters, then park it around by the side entrance to the Files Office. Leave the motor running and clear out. Can you do that?"

"Yes, Cal, but—"

"I'm not telling you any more," said Cal. "If you have to ask questions, don't do it."

"All right," she said. "Give me a minute to get somebody up here to take over the ward desk."

Cal drove a ground car of his own to Expedition HQ. In the scope he could see Annie's car following. He pulled into the official parking lot, and went in.

"Colonel?" said the Wing Section behind the small wooden fence that separated staff from visitors in the outer office.

"Contacts Service," said Cal. "Colonel Truant. I'm to talk to General Harmon." And without waiting for an answer, he pushed open the small gate in the fence and strode past.

"But Colonel, just a minute. *Colonel!*"

He heard steps behind him but kept going. He passed through another door into another, smaller office, where a Captain looked up, startled, from a wide desk.

"Colonel Truant!" said Cal. He kept traveling. The farther door in this second office was closed. He opened it and stepped through.

Harmon and Colonel Alt were standing together by a desk, within.

They both turned as the Captain from the outer office and other staff members reached the door behind Cal.

"General," said Cal. "I think it's time for your talk with the Contacts Services."

"I'm sorry, sir," said the Captain, from behind Cal's shoulder. "He just walked by—"

"That's all right," said Harmon. "Close the door." Cal heard them leave and the door close behind him.

"Alone," said Cal.

Colonel Haga Alt came around the desk, walking on his toes like a boxer.

"Truant," he said, "I've waited one hell of a long time for—"

"Hag," said Harmon. Alt stopped. He looked back at Harmon. "It's all right, Hag," said Harmon gently. "You can leave us."

Alt's nostrils spread. "All right, sir," he said. He walked on, looking squarely into Cal's face, passed him, and Cal heard the door shut a second time behind him.

"All right, Truant," said Harmon, in the same gentle voice. "What is it?"

"The Paumons are rising."

"I know," said Harmon.

"I know you know," said Cal. "I know you planned it this way. There was a time when I thought you just didn't know any better. But I found out different."

Harmon walked around the desk himself and stood in front of it. They were only a few feet apart. Harmon put his hands together behind him, like a lecturer.

"Back in Denver," he said, "I sent you to General Scoby because I was under the impression that whatever had happened to you with the Lehaunan, you were a soldier."

"I was," said Cal. "I was one of the prettiest."

"But you aren't any more?"

"Yes," said Cal. "I'm a soldier. I'm a hell of a soldier. But maybe you wouldn't recognize the kind I am."

"No," Harmon said. "You're wrong. I would recognize what kind you are. In fact, I do. That's why I'm talking to you, instead of having you thrown out." He sat down on the edge of the desk. "You're the best kind, Cal. That's why I sent you over to Scoby in the first place. Because you're the kind that has to fight out of a sense of conviction. Men like that are too valuable to lose."

"Only, I am wrong."

"Yes," said Harmon. "You got in among people like General Scoby who talk about fine things like peace and understanding and no more war. It impressed you. I think you may have forgotten that those sort of things don't come about naturally. They have to be imposed by a strong hand from the outside." He looked at Cal, and his voice was almost pleading. "I want you to understand. Damn it, you're the sort of man who *ought* to understand."

"I should, should I?" said Cal.

"Yes. Because you've seen both sides of it. You're not like these half-baked glory-preachers that think we're going to have Heaven next Tuesday. I tell you, Cal, I've got more use for a Prog like Wantaki, than I have for these Societics-Contacts choirboys."

"It's mutual, no doubt," said Cal. "You're both generals."

Harmon frowned at him.

"Something in particular seems to be eating on you," he said.

"Major Blye's dead—you know, Zone Eleven. I brought his body back with me."

"I didn't know. That's too bad," said Harmon. "There's a man who was a soldier clear through. I'll bet he died like one."

"He sure did," said Cal.

"I want to hear how it happened. But the point right now is something different: You, not Major Blye, good man though he was. I'm fighting for your soul, Cal. Do you believe I'm an honest man? Tell me."

"Yes," said Cal. "I believe you're honest. I believe you believe every word you say."

"Then believe me when I say nobody wants peace more than I. That I agree with Scoby one hundred per cent about these Paumons being the nearest thing to human we've ever run across, with brains and soul and pain-reactions to match. He's told you that? I see he has. But from that point he gets idealistic, and I get practical. He thinks this qualifies them to be great friends. I know it qualifies them to be great enemies. It's one thing to make a pet out of a dog; but don't try to make one out of a wolf."

"Or a cheetah?" said Cal.

Harmon stopped talking. The whites of his eyes showed a little.

"I'm talking seriously," he said.

"So am I," said Cal. "Don't you know why that cheetah does things for Scoby?"

"I don't know and I don't care," said Harmon. "I'm concerned with the future of two races, not with a brainless animal. I'm concerned with making you see that just because these Paumons are what they are—because they're so much like us—that we can't ever trust them. We've started something and we can't stop now. Now we've got to break them; teach them with a blood-bath that they'll remember to the ultimate generations, that the human is master. We can't stop now."

"Why'd we start in the first place?"

"History," said Harmon, "forced our hand. We're an expanding people." He stood up. "Cal," he said, "can't you see that what I've arranged for isn't only the right thing, it's the most humanitarian thing? We treated the Paumons humanly in the original conquest. Because of that they took the enough rope we gave them and now they're going to hang themselves. They, themselves, are insisting on being taught a lesson. And, like a good surgeon, I save lives by cutting now instead of later, when a more extensive operation would be necessary. I save human lives. You might say, I even save Paumons lives. Because, if they grew to a real threat to us, we might have to exterminate them completely."

"Yeah," said Cal.

"You understand, then," said Harmon. "Believe me, Cal. You were one of the ones I had hoped could understand."

"No," said Cal. "Put me down with Scoby. No, put me down a notch below Scoby, because I'm still ready to fight and kill if I have to, in spite of this shoulder patch. I just don't have to pretend there's anything right or noble about it."

Harmon sighed. He shook his head slowly.

"I'm sorry, Cal," he said.

"So am I," said Cal. "I just finished talking to Wantaki. I told him he could come in here with sufficient force to protect himself. Then he could talk over this Paumons situation—not as conquered talking to conquerer, but as a couple of equals meeting face to face, with the object of avoiding any more fighting. I gave him my promise."

"That was foolish," said Harmon. "It was even a little ridiculous."

"No," said Cal. "Because as Contacts Service Head on this planet, I'm interdicting any military action by the Expedition during the time of the talk."

"I see," said Harmon. He stood for a moment, then turned to the desk behind him and pressed a button. Holding it down, he spoke to the desk. "Will you send in a couple of Military Police?" he said. He let up the button and turned back to Cal. "As I say," he said. "I'm sorry. I would rather have made an ally of you than arrested you."

"Yes," said Cal.

He hit Harmon suddenly in the stomach, and, as the other man fell toward him, hit him again behind the ear with the side of his hand. Harmon fell to the floor and lay there quietly. Cal went out through the back door of the office, down a flight of stairs and into another office banked with the metal cases of microfiles.

"Sit still, sit still," he said to the startled workers there. "Just taking the short way to my car."

He went out a further door onto the street. The car Annie had been driving was parked across from him. He sprinted for it. As he dived inside behind the control stick, he heard someone shout from the door he had just come through.

He floored the throttle and the car jumped away from the Headquarters Building. He shot down the street, out onto the road to the Expedition Landing field and pulled up at the base of the towering flagship. Thirty feet up the service ramp, the rear port was open to the ventilation of the warming day. He was through the hatch and throwing over the hand control to close and lock the port when he heard somebody breathing hard behind him.

He turned. It was Annie.

"You crazy fool!" he said.

The port slammed shut and locked with a clang. A second later the inner door closed also.

Chapter Sixteen

———◆———

"You've got to get out of here," said Cal. "You don't know what you're in to."

"I won't," said Annie. "I know very well. And I won't. You can't put me out bodily, either, without leaving the controls here. And you can't risk that."

"I'll manage it."

"No," said Annie. She was quite pale. "I won't let you. I can fight that hard."

They were up in the observation room, where the standby controls of the ship were. The duty caretaker was locked in the projection room behind the wall chart. Cal had the stand-by power on. It did not take an engineer to do that much; and the housekeeping energy flow it gave him was all he needed. Outside, above the entry ports at three levels, the red lights were glowing to warn anyone back beyond a hundred-yard circle. From the outside screen Cal could see the field below, and the other ships like models, the little buildings of the field, and Headquarters, the hospital, and beyond those buildings the limits of Manaha. Beyond this he could see the green and open hills, with here and there the darker green of trees.

The ground phone buzzed. Cal answered, and the screen lit up with the face of Colonel Alt.

"Truant," he said. "Come out of that ship before I send in MP's to haul you out."

"I wouldn't try that if I were you," said Cal. "I'm prepared to blow this ship and half the plateau if I have to."

Alt hesitated. He looked aside for a moment, then back into the screen.

"You'd do better to cooperate," he said. "I'd be justified in having you shot on sight. You killed General Harmon when you hit him."

"Don't lie to me, Colonel," said Cal. "I know when I kill a man. Tell the General I want to talk to him as soon as he's up to it."

He cut the connection. He sat down in the operator's chair by the little desk below the screens. His head swam; his body felt several gravities heavy. He put his head down for a second on his arms and immediately felt Annie shaking him.

"Lie down," she was saying. "There's an off-watch cot in the Communications Room. Here . . ." She was tugging him to his feet. "You've got to rest. When did you sleep last?"

"No—" he said. And all the time, he felt his will-less, stupid body being steered by Annie toward the cot. "Harmon'll call back. . . ."

"Let him call. I'll answer."

"No. You get out. . . ." The words were thick on his tongue. The edge of the cot struck under his knees, and he fell into it. The world made a sort of half-turn around him, as if he were very drunk. And then it suddenly winked out.

His head hurt. It was the amber light from the barber poles, street lights of the Lehaunan town, that was dazzling his eyes and giving him a headache. And he had never been so tired. He wandered through the town with his fire rifle in his hands, letting his feet take him among the dome-shaped buildings. Now and then he shot perfunctorily at what might be Lehaunans. He was so tired that he could not think exactly what he was doing there. Something had not worked out, and he had decided to do something else. But just at the moment he could not remember what that was. He was tired and looking for a place to sit down.

He came at last to a little open space between the buildings, and there was one of the small protuberances like a half-barrel sticking up out of the pavement. He sat down on it and rested his fire rifle across his knees.

There was a building a little to his right and another a little farther off, up ahead of him and to his left. Almost directly ahead, about thirty yards away, was a third building. A barber pole by the building to his right spread its crackling light impartially over the scene.

He sat, not thinking of anything, and after a little while, a Lehaunan ran across the open space before him, saw him, hesitated, and then ran on. A little later, he saw another one run between two houses farther off that could be seen dimly beyond the building to his left.

He did not move. He felt a sort of numb oneness with his surroundings, as if he had grown to be part of the object he was sitting on. The thought that was in his head, like a title on a movie screen frozen in position, was that if he rested for a little while he would remember what he was to do next. He sat still.

Some little time later, a family of three came out of the building directly before him, out of its triangular-shaped entrance. They were evidently an adult male, a female adult a little smaller, and a small young one. He sat so still that they were only about a dozen feet from him when they saw him, and stopped short. They were carrying some small packages.

He and they remained motionless, staring at each other.

It's quite all right, he said inside his head, in normal human speech, *go ahead. I won't bother you.* It was too much effort to say the words aloud. So, having said them mentally, he merely continued to sit there.

The female adult made a small noise and pushed slightly at the young one. The youngster hesitated; she pushed again. Reluctantly the young one ran off, past Cal and out of sight. The two adults stayed facing him.

That's all right, he said in his head. *You go, too. You're obviously civilians. Besides, I have taken your town. I've got no need to shoot you.*

They did not move for a moment. Then, as if they had heard his thoughts, they began to back cautiously away from him.

There, you see? he thought. *You're quite safe. I'm not going to do anything.* They were like ants, he thought; afraid of being stepped on. He watched them back away. They were quite handsome in their black fur. He must look like a monster to them. An incomprehensible monster that killed or did not kill for no sane reason.

Still holding their packages, they were backing away from him, back toward the house from which they had come. Sudden pity flooded him.

Go in peace, he thought. *Go in safety.*

They were almost halfway across the open space between him and the house, now. The male turned and, turning the female, urged her in front of him. They broke suddenly into a run for their own doorway.

They're getting away, thought Cal suddenly.

He raised his rifle and shot the male, who fell immediately. The female dropped her packages and put on speed. His second shot dropped her just inside the doorway. He could see her lying there.

The packages lay scattered about in the open. He

wondered, idly, what sort of valuables might be in them. They should be saved, he thought, so the young one could claim them at some future date. . . .

Annie was shaking him. It was a terribly hard thing to wake up. He struggled into a sitting position on the side of the cot, but he had come to with only half his mind. The other half was still back in the circumstances he had been reliving in the dream.

". . . General Harmon," Annie was saying. "He wants to talk to you. I didn't want to wake you, but you've been sleeping there almost nine hours."

"Nine hours!" He staggered to his feet and lurched into the observation room. Annie made to help him to the ground phone, but he shook his head. "He can wait." He laid sleep-numbed hands on the controls of the outside screen. It was late afternoon now and on the far hills, the light of Bellatrix had turned the covering moss to chartreuse color, and the clumped trees to a deeper green. He ran the magnification up to the limits of the scale and saw, as from a dozen or so yards away, armed Paumons soldiers standing under the trees.

"Wantaki," he said. "He made it."

"What?" said Annie.

He did not answer, swinging across the room to the ground phone. He punched the receive button, and the image of General Harmon sprang to life on the screen. He was standing half-turned away from Cal. The call buzzer at the other end must have sounded then, for Harmon turned back and approached the screen. He looked as calm and unharmed as ever.

"Colonel Truant," he said quietly, "I'm ordering you to come out of that ship."

"No," said Cal. His legs were still weak from sleep. He sat down in front of the screen. "I'm staying here until you commit yourself to a meeting with Wantaki, by letting him into the Headquarters area with enough men to match your Headquarters forces."

"I'm not the kind of man you can blackmail, Colonel," said Harmon.

"I'm not blackmailing you," said Cal. "I'm holding you up with a loaded gun at your head. If I blow this ship, you, Wantaki and everything goes. If it goes, there's nothing left of the Expedition on this world but a lot of small scattered garrisons. They wouldn't last twenty-four hours with the real power of the outfit destroyed here."

"Rather a strange way to go about saving lives, isn't it?" said Harmon gently. "Have you counted the people that'll die—the Paumons, as well—if you blow up that ship and its armaments?"

"You don't understand me," said Cal. "I told you I wasn't up on General Scoby's level. I know what I am, if I blow this ship. But if I have to blow it the Paumons'll come out of it better than if I hadn't. The only way I can get you to meet with them properly is to threaten to blow it. And I can't threaten it without meaning it. And I mean it, General!" Cal looked into the imaged eyes of Harmon, but what he saw was a small black-furred figure tugging and murmuring at a larger, black-furred figure fallen still in a triangular doorway. "You better believe I mean it."

"I'll give you thirty minutes," said Harmon. "If you haven't started to come out thirty minutes from now, I'll order the other ships on the field here to open fire on you."

"You know," said Cal, "you can't destroy this ship before I can blow it. And you're just as liable to blow it yourself trying to destroy it. I'll give you until sunset, about two hours. If Wantaki and his men aren't entering the Headquarters area by sunset, I'll blow the ship."

"Thirty minutes," said Harmon.

"Good by," said Cal. He cut the connection. He stood up, turned, and saw Annie standing a little across the room from him.

"Annie," he said, "there's an escape pod in the nose of this ship that'll kick itself fifty miles up and six hundred miles out. You get in it and get out of here."

"No," said Annie. "I told you I wouldn't."

"I am too dead to argue with you. Don't you understand? Two hours from now, I'm going to press that arming connection and destroy every living thing for five hundred miles. Can't you get that through your head? I'm going to have to do it!"

"The General will give in."

"No, he won't," said Cal. He looked grimly at the blank screen of the ground phone. "He can't. Not while there's a chance I might not press the button. And by the time he knows for sure there's no chance, it'll be too late."

"I'll wait till the last minute," said Annie. "But I won't go a second before."

Cal felt suddenly weak all over. He realized suddenly he had been standing with every muscle tensed to the limit, as if he had crossed his fingers with all the strength in his body, against the possibility that she would refuse to go and he could not get her out before the end.

He let out his breath suddenly and sat down in the chair.

"Good," he said. "Good."

She came quickly over to him.

"Cal," she said, "are you all right?"

"Fine," he said. "Fine." She had her arms around him. He grinned a little shakily and reached up and patted one of the arms that held him. "It's just that I love you." The words came out quite easily. He had never been able to say them before. He said them again. "I love you."

She held on to him. They did not say much. After a little while she excused herself and was gone for a few moments. And then she came back and they sat together, watching the sun moving toward the horizon.

When it touched the tops of the hills, he felt a strange, cold, feeling thrill suddenly all the way through him. He turned to her.

"It's time," he said.

She did not move.

"You've got to go now," he said.

"I lied to you," she said. "I never planned to go. When I went out just now, I went up to the pod and smashed the control board. I couldn't leave if I wanted to."

He could only stare at her.

"Don't you see?" she said, almost composedly, "I *want* to stay with you."

He said, through stiff lips:

"I can't blow it with you here."

"Yes, you can," she said. Her voice was very quiet, very certain. It was as if she had moved into a shell of peace from which nothing would be able to take her, neither death nor sorrow. "I know you can."

He got heavily to his feet, and looked once more to the hills. The light of the sun was now resting on them and it made the whole horizon seem ablaze with horizontal rays shooting all at him. He walked slowly over to the arming button. He looked at her again and put his finger on it.

"All right, Cal," said a voice from somewhere above his head. "You win."

It was the voice of Harmon. Cal stared foolishly around, for a second he half-expected the General to walk into the observation room.

"We've been listening to you," said Harmon. "We fired a contact mike into the skin of your ship eight hours ago. If you'd left that room for five minutes, we'd have had you. Look out to the hills, there. I've had Alt standing by to pass the word to Wantaki. You can see the Progs already starting to come in."

Cal looked. Against the glare of the sun he had to shield his eyes. But when he did he made out dark masses moving in, close to Manaha. They were already in below the range of Headquarters heavy ground weapons.

"All right," said Cal. "I'll come down."

He waited until the approaching Paumons forces were actually into the city. Then he went down in the ship, with Annie beside him. When they stepped out onto the ramp and started to the ground, he saw that there was quite a gathering waiting for them. There were Military Police, both male and female, Colonel Harry Adom of the Military Police, and Cal's own Contacts Service aide, Major Kai. Major Kai was fifteen years older than Cal and looked like a bank clerk. He represented the old guard over whose head Scoby had put Cal in charge. Kai was looking embarrassed and unhappy, but Cal was glad to see him there.

"Major," he said. "You take over Contacts until orders can be got out from General Scoby. He'll want—"

"He's here, himself," interrupted Kai. "Or rather, he's coming in right now." He pointed off to their left and upward. Cal, glancing in that direction, saw the sudden flash of a pinpoint of reflecting surface, high enough up to still catch the sunlight.

"When did he send word he was coming?" said Cal.

"Yesterday," said Kai unhappily. "The message came in. We couldn't get hold of you."

Cal had reached the bottom of the ramp now. The MP's waiting there closed about him. He saw the female MP's moving in on Annie.

"Wait a minute!" he called. "She didn't have anything to do with this. I—"

They paid no attention to him. The MP's were searching him for weapons.

"All clean," said one.

Across the field, the courier ship bearing Scoby was now down and landed. There was quite a crowd around it, and as the hatch opened and the small figure preceded by a small cheetah came out, another small figure walking like Harmon stepped forward to shake hands.

"Cal," said Annie's voice.

He looked over at her, as the cold metal of handcuffs closed around his wrists. They were doing the same thing to her. For a second, they could look at each other. Then the MP's closed around Cal once more and he and she were led off in different directions.

Chapter Seventeen

The Military Police took Cal to the Stockade and locked him in a cell by himself in an unoccupied section of the building. It was so quiet and isolated that it was almost as if he were in a hospital instead of a prison. At the end of four days they took him in a closed car to the field and put him on a ship for Earth. It was impossible to tell what had happened since he had been arrested. Fighting might even have been going on without his being able to know it. And they made it a point to tell him nothing. Scoby did not come to see him.

Back at Earth, he was taken to the Fort Shuttleworth

Military Prison outside Denver and housed in separate quarters that were a little better than a cell—a room and a half. It was like a small, compact apartment, and through the bars of a fairly wide window Cal could see a section of perfectly kept green lawn, some tall, pyramidal pine trees, and beyond that the white top of a mountain. He thought that it was Longs Peak, but he could not be sure and a small, irrational stubbornness kept him from asking anyone, so he never did establish its identity from that window for certain.

Shortly after he was placed there, a Captain from the Adjutant General's department came to see him with a folder of papers. The Captain identified himself as Cal's legal representative. He explained something to the effect that they were pondering charges against Cal. It would probably be treason and lesser crimes, but nothing was established yet. For some reason it was a matter of jurisdiction. The Captain took himself and his work very seriously, and most of what he had to say Cal found fairly unintelligible. The Captain wanted an account in Cal's own words of what had led up to Cal's arrest, and took it down in recorder and on paper. He and Cal were pretty well up against it as far as the book went, he told Cal. They would find it hard to deny the statements of prosecution. Their best bet, considering the Lehaunan background, might be to make their claim one of temporary insanity.

Cal was uncooperative on that point. He would not claim temporary insanity. Otherwise, he paid only slight attention to the Captain's flow of words. He was more interested in pumping the other man for news. Annie, said the Captain, was under arrest elsewhere. He did not know exactly where. He, himself, was not representing her. About the Paumons, he had very little information. The human and native Alien forces there were certainly at peace at the present moment, though the situation was touchy, as always. Yes, he believed the Paumons authorities had had some sort of official talk with the human Command, but there had been no more than a mention of it in the news services and he had heard nothing from official sources.

"It's a long ways off, there around Bellatrix, you know," he said to Cal.

After the Captain's visit, they began to allow Cal the news services and he got a sudden supply of backed-up mail. There was nothing from Scoby and only a handful of letters from Annie—and these had been censored almost into unintelligibility. Cal wrote her back, but with no great hopes that his letters would not be treated the same way.

It was July on Earth. There were seldom clouds on the mountain peak Cal could see from his window. He read a good deal and thought and walked around his locked quarters. The Captain came occasionally with papers for him to fill out or sign. July went into August and August drifted into September. He felt the leaking away of the valuable days of his life. He had found again the serenity that had come to him in the later days of Contacts School, and he did not worry too whole-heartedly over what would eventually happen to him. It was a curious thing that while the death penalty was not now imposed by a civilian court, the Armed Services had retained it for certain crimes. For himself, his conscience was clear and it was no worse an end than Walk's had been. But he worried about what would be done to Annie.

Then, the third week in September, his Captain was able to tell him that Annie had been released without charges. He felt a great relief and even hoped that she might manage to visit him after that. But she did not come, and even her letters stopped coming. He told himself that this was good, that she was well out of it.

He was able to face the fact that he loved her now, and understand why he had been unable to tell her so before. He had been shackled by the old fear of a re-enactment of his mother's death, with Annie in his mother's role, and he in his father's. Just so, he had been able to face the fact that he had always wanted to be the sort of man his father was, but had gone against him because he had blamed his father for his mother's death. Looking at his father through the stripped eyes of a child, he had taken his father's refusal to be vindictive against the Armed Services and the officer indirectly responsible for his wife's death, as a sign his father did not really *care*. Now that his father was dead, it came to Cal that his father must have cared very much.

Not only cared, but loved!—and been right about many things. He had been right about the uncertainty of that thin line that marks off the soldier from the murderer, that thin line that is also the edge of the precipice over which the spirit of a man falls to its final destruction. Cal could face this, too, now, as he could face the fact that with the Lehaunan in that village he himself had crossed the line and fallen. A man, he told himself now, can kill and go on living. But if he murders, he erects a barrier between himself and life; a barrier behind which he dies alone.

And a man begins, thought Cal, to murder when he begins to tell himself that it is all right to kill; that there are practical or moral justifications for it. Because there are none. Sometimes it happens and things afterwards are better than they were before. But it is never good, it is always bad. There was always a better way if someone had had the wit to find it.

I suppose, thought Cal, leaning against his window and looking out through the bars at the grass and the pines swayed by the wind that seemed to be always blowing, and the far-off mountain peak with a small white cloud near it—I suppose it should be pushed right to the point of holding insects and microbes sacred, to hold water. But that's a trap, too. To say, if I can't be perfect there's no point in my being good at all. I didn't have any qualms back there on the Paumons about blowing up Harmon—no, of course I did. But the point is: how much more readily I would have put my own head on the block to pull Walk out. And Harmon by his own standards is an upright and honorable man, while Walk was something to frighten Paumons babies with and better off dead.

No, Cal corrected himself again, I'm wrong about that. Nobody is better off dead, not in that sense. No. There are always miracles. There is always hope. If you deny miracles and hope, you're playing God—and that's the insects and microbes bit all over again. If I can't shoot par, I won't pick up a golf club. Wrong. You stick by what you believe, and go on doing what you can in your own clumsy, imperfect way, trying to hack out Heaven by next Tuesday, even though practical people like Harmon are sure it can't be done. And damned if you don't make some progress now and then.

Christ, yes, thought Cal! Otherwise we might as well have stayed in little family ape-bands, wandering around and trying to tear out the throat of every other living thing that stood up to us. The thing is not to kid yourself. Just because cutting a man open to get out his ruptured appendix has a way of saving his life doesn't mean that it's a good thing to cut a man open. It's a very bad thing, a destructive, immoral wrong being done to the living body. And you must never lose sight of that fact, either through long custom or need to justify your own emotional reactions to the cutting. And one day you may be moved to the point of finding some way to save the man's life without cutting him open.

And it's that way with us, thought Cal. We mustn't lose sight of the fact that it's wrong to go up against each new race we meet with all guns blazing. The only right way in the end is to go naked to the stars. Without weapons, because we don't need them. You never find a way until you try. And you don't try as long as you kid yourself that it's okay to—

The sound of a door opening behind him broke off Cal's train of thought. It was one of his guards with the noon meal on a tray.

"No mail today either," said the guard, as he put the tray down. "They seem to be losing your address these last few weeks."

Two weeks later, Cal was taken from his cell to the office of the Director of the Prison, where an Administrative Services Captain told him he was released. There was no explanation. He was given a small plastic container in which to carry his possessions, a sealed manila envelope, and escorted to the gate of the Prison.

As he walked to the gate, he opened the envelope and drew out a sheet of paper inside. It was his release from the Services. He was discharged, he read, without honor but with prejudice, and not recommended for reservice. The gate opened before him and he stepped out into the wide parking lot beyond.

He had to look twice to believe what he saw. It was Annie, and Scoby with the cheetah, and beyond them a convertible flyer. Annie ran and put her arms around him, but Scoby stood impatiently with one foot on the step to the open door of the flyer.

"Oh, Cal!" said Annie, holding tightly to him. "Cal, will you ever forgive us? We couldn't. We just couldn't!"

"Come on, come on!" said Scoby.

They got into the flyer and Scoby sat down at the controls with Annie and Cal on the curved seat behind him. Annie would not let go of Cal; she sat pressed close against him.

"Oh, Cal!" she said. She was trying not to cry and it was making her nose red.

Scoby touched the controls and the flyer went straight up about nine thousand feet, then made a half-turn and streaked eastward. Cal caught one last glimpse of the mountain peak to the north of his prison window. It apparently had put aside all clouds in honor of the occasion. It stood sharp and white against the perfect blue of the sky.

"Where are we going?" asked Cal.

"Washington," grunted Scoby

"Darling," said Annie. "We couldn't even write. We had to make them think you weren't at all important, that we'd forgotten all about you."

Cal shook his head. The whole thing had happened so quickly everything had an unnatural feel to it, as if it was a trick of some sort.

"But what happened?" he said.

"Politics," said Scoby, not turning his head. Limpari swung cat's eyes about from where she sat staring out the window, and then yawned at Scoby.

"He had to wait. I had to wait, too. Until it looked as if nobody cared what happened to you any more. That's why I stopped writing you. Only I didn't stop writing, Cal. I wrote anyway. I just didn't mail the letters. I've got them all for you."

The flyer had been continuing to climb and to increase its speed as it did so. They were now at a hundred thousand feet with the sky black overhead. Their speed would be about two thousand miles an hour, Cal noted automatically from the instruments before Scoby. After sitting still for so many weeks it was an odd sensation to have sprouted wings and be hurtling to some distant destination. Below him, he could see the line of the sunset, flowing toward them across the earth below. He felt the beginnings of a slow return from numbness, like a leg that has gone to sleep and is just now beginning to wake up.

"I thought you were well out of it," he said to Annie.

"Oh, *no!*" she said. "You knew I'd never just give you up. You knew Walt would never abandon you, either!"

"Walt?" he said. And then he remembered that this was Scoby's first name. It was a small shock, after all this, to realize Scoby had a first name. "I don't understand. I don't understand it," Cal said. "That Captain assigned to my case said the charge was probably going to be treason." He looked at Scoby. "And here I am."

"Matter of jurisdiction," said Scoby. The ship had leveled off now. He put it on automatic pilot and swiveled his chair around, pulling out his pipe. "That's what I went back about. The time was just right for squeezing on the home front. I squeezed." He got the pipe going. "I got the Contacts Service made a separate civilian branch. Not under Armed Services any more."

"So you were really acting under civilian authority when you interdicted Harmon and tried to make him talk with Wantaki," said Annie. "Even if you didn't know it, or Harmon didn't."

Cal looked from one to the other.

"What difference did that make?" he said.

"Just one," answered Scoby, uttering rich puffs of smoke from his pipe. "Harmon didn't have the authority to order you arrested. On paper, since a peace had been signed with the Paumons, you as head of the Contacts *Department,* were his superior, not he yours."

Scoby leaned back around to the automatic pilot and set the speed-and-distance clock.

"Of course," he said, swinging back to face them, "he had a case to make. The fact orders hadn't arrived; and you threatened human as well as Paumons lives, and so forth. So what I did was wait and let things cool, until it wasn't worth the Combat Services' while to make an issue out of you. Early this week I tacked your release onto a list of little minor demands I was dealing with from the Services. And here you are."

Cal sighed. He felt abruptly small, and insignificant.

"No fuss," said Scoby. "Or wasn't that what you were thinking?"

"Not exactly," said Cal. He looked ahead out the window of the flyer. They were almost to their meeting with the sunset line moving toward them over the relief map of the earth below, and beyond that edge of light he saw only darkness. "I was thinking it's all over, now."

"Over?" said Scoby.

"Finished! Wound up," said Cal.

"Finished!" said Scoby. "What d'you mean *finished?* You think you brought eternal peace to the Paumons by having Wantaki and Harmon hating each other's guts?"

"No," said Cal, "they admire each other."

"Hating each other's guts and admiring each other, what the hell's the difference," said Scoby. "But just the two of them sitting down across a table from each other? You think the Lehaunan're all set up, now, or there's no rebuilding to be done with the Griella? That what you think?"

"No," said Cal. There was a slow, heavy weariness creeping into him. He was looking out the window now at the rapidly approaching darkness—and remembering. It seemed there was always a darkness for him. It had been dark on the Lehaunan hillside before they had gone in to take the town. It had been in darkness that Walk had called him a Gutless Wonder; and in the Paumons darkness, Walk had died. Night had been falling as he reached for the arming button on the flagship, that meant the end for everyone there; and darkness was falling again, here, now.

"Don't you think there's work to be done?" Scoby was saying. "Why do you think I worked so hard to get you loose? This is what I've been after from the start. My own Department, independent, where I can get the kind of men I want and train them the way they ought to be trained, instead of having to let good people go by the board because they couldn't pass Services' physical, or couldn't make it over an obstacle course!" He glared at Cal.

"What do you think I've been driving at all this time, but an army of my own—a Contacts army which'll go on growing and getting more effective until the Combat Services can't do without us? Until we get so good at last, that the day comes they let us go in *first,* to see if we can't make it without fighting at all. *That's* what I've been working for all these years. *That's* when I'm going to need the sort of men this race of ours has only written philosophies about before. *That's* why I want you—for my right hand man, to take over for me when the time comes—just as I planned it from the first time I discovered you."

The twilight line was under and past them, now. It was all a dark world ahead.

"It's no use," said Cal. He leaned forward and passed his manila envelope to Scoby. "I'm discharged with prejudice. Not recommended for reservice."

Scoby slammed the envelope to the floor of the flyer.

"Bonehead!" he snarled. *"Department,* I said. Not Service! You had so many coats of varnish you think that if the Services turn you down, the Civilian Departments can't hire you either?"

Cal lifted his head, startled.

"I thought—Government—" he began, and got stuck.

"Oh, the personnel don't like hiring Service bad cases. They don't *like* hiring ex-cons or reformed alcoholics, either. But I'm in charge of my Department. And *I* say you're hired. And you're hired!"

Cal sat, letting some of the sense of it sink in.

"I want men!" Scoby was muttering furiously. "Men, not recommendations on paper!" He was simply blowing off the last of his head of steam. As proof of the fact, he was glaring not at Cal, but ahead out the windscreen of the flyer. "Christ! it's hard enough to handle things as it is. It's hard enough to do the job I have to do—and that's double the job I ought to be doing at my age—with the sort of men I want, anyway. Let alone . . ."

Cal looked ahead out of the flyer's windscreen, himself. Annie was sitting close beside him and had slipped an arm through his left arm. He felt the living and continual warmth of her body, close. A sort of hope stirred in him. The thrumming vibrations of the flyer hummed through him down to the furthest tips of his fingers. He could feel the lift of the ship's wide wings, spread now at this altitude to their greatest, hawk-like, soaring dimensions, bearing him up. On those wings they here in this ship sailed against the night, at speeds of which no flint-axed caveman had ever dreamed.

Far up ahead, on the darkened horizon, a sprinkling of lights rose into view around the curve of the world. They rose and multiplied as the flyer dropped toward them, until they looked like jewels of all colors scattered more and more thickly upon a cloth of black velvet. Together, the spectrum of their many-colored rays made up the white light of a city. It was the city toward which he and Annie and Scoby—all of them together in the flyer—were now heading above the primitive darkness, as to an inevitable destination.

And to that city, now, they stooped.